Peacetalk 101

by Suzette Haden Elgin

2003

Copyright © 2003 Suzette Haden Elgin

This paperback edition first published in 2003 by Lethe Press

ISBN 1-59021-030-1

Manufactured in the United States of America

Visit the Peacetalk 101 homepage at http://www.sfwa.org/members/elgin/Peacetalk101/Index.html

Cover design and text page formats by Bill Patton

102 Heritage Avenue, Maple Shade, NJ 08052
lethepress@aol.com

This book is for Ben.

Ben Elgin
1966-1995

FOREWORD

This is the story of a man, and what happened to him, and what he did about it. His name was Henry, and he had a hard row to hoe. His first thought when he woke up every morning was "Here we go again — and I can't *face* it!" But of course no matter how many mornings he started out like that, he had to face it anyway. That's the way things are.

Henry had a wife and a child, and neither one of them was what he had expected; he was pretty sure he wasn't what *they* had expected either. He had a dog that wouldn't come when he called it, and a car that only started about half the time. He had friends who didn't show him the respect he deserved, and an elderly mother who was getting vague and weepy and didn't recognize him when he went to see her, and a nosy father-in-law who lived much too close by; he had a greedy Congressman who was no more use than the dog. He lived in a rented house that was hot in the summer and cold in the winter and always felt like it was closing in on him. He had a job that he hated but was afraid to leave, because it was a pretty good job and good jobs aren't easy to find. He had a bad back and he caught bad colds, and he weighed twenty pounds too many. He was an ordinary man, with an ordinary man's problems. That didn't please him; he had thought he'd do a lot better than that.

He believed in God, but he didn't *trust* God; it seemed to Henry that God was unreliable and absentminded. And of course there was the crazy weather; he didn't know *what* to make of *it.*

However, Henry felt as though he might have been able to put up with all those things if that had been the end of it. What he couldn't bear, somehow, what seemed to him to be the last straw, was that he had no *peace,* and as far as he could tell, neither did anybody else.

Everywhere he went, it was the same. Everybody bickering and badmouthing and putting each other down; everybody nagging and griping and sneering, whining and carping and bellyaching. Everybody out to win the award for Wickedest Mouth In The East, and Meanest Mouth In The West, and Foulest Mouth Overall. And they were *proud* of it! It baffled him, the way they behaved. Everybody wading around up to their noses in what looked and sounded and smelled to Henry like a cesspool of talk, and so proud of their performance that they couldn't stop bragging. It was "Boy, I really got *her* going, *didn't* I?" and 'Hey, did you see the way I made him *squirm?* How *about* that! Am I a great communicator or *what?*" and "It'll be a cold day in *hell* before they take *me* on again!" On top of everything else he had to put up with, it was too much. Way too much.

The day finally came when Henry had had all he could stand. He wanted out. He decided that he would do two more weeks of this hard row of his, so there'd be one more paycheck and he could leave with his bills mostly paid, and then he was going to hoe no more; he was going to get out of this mess for good. He had no rich relatives to wait around for, and he knew the Publishers Clearing House guys weren't going to be stopping by his place. Death was the only door that was open to him; he was going to go through that door. And because they were his responsibility and there was no one he could count on to look after them, he would be taking the wife and the child with him. He hadn't yet decided exactly how he was going to work it all out, because thinking about it made him sick at his stomach. But his mind was made up. Two more weeks — and then, **Lights Out**.

Henry was ordinary, but he wasn't stupid. He did realize that a man with only two weeks left in his life ought to do or say at least a few significant things in the time that remained to him. He even sat himself down and deliberately tried to think of something significant to do. But nothing came to him. His mind, which had been so little use in his life so far, was no use to him this time either; it stayed as blank and empty as water in a ditch on a gray day. And so he just went on about his business the way he always had, to make the time go by.

PEACETALK 101

CHAPTER ONE

On this particular sticky summer day, Henry had tried and failed to get his car started, and he'd had to take the bus to work. He was hot and cross and weary by the time he started home, and he sat down in the last empty window seat and stared out through the dirty glass. He had the idea that at least for this twenty-five minute bus ride he wouldn't have to hear any poisonous talk that was aimed straight at him. There'd be the usual abundance of the stuff all around him, sure; but it wouldn't have anything to do with him. Because he was looking forward to the break, his heart sank when, at the very last instant, just as the bus was pulling away from the curb, a homeless person scrambled on board and sat down beside him.

The bus had filled up completely; there was nowhere for Henry to move to. He gritted his teeth and kept his head turned hard to the window, and closed his eyes. Maybe the person would have the decency to leave him alone?

It didn't turn out that way; Henry wasn't surprised. The homeless man spoke right up. "Hello there," he said, "and a good afternoon to you!"

"Mmmmmmmm...gub," Henry mumbled, doing his best to signal *I'm asleep, you turkey, can't you tell I'm asleep?*

"People who sleep on the bus sleep past their stop," came the reply. "You tell me where you want off, I'll wake you up when we get there."

Henry's eyes opened, and then narrowed; this was like when you stop for a red light and the homeless kid comes over to wash your windshield.

"No, thanks!" he said firmly.

"You're going all the way and back, like me?"

It meant "You're homeless, you've got no place to lay your head or keep your stuff, like me? You spend your time riding around on buses all day, like me?"

Henry cleared his throat. "No," he said. You didn't ever want to say one more word to these people than you absolutely had to say.

"So you just don't care if you miss your stop?"

"No. I don't care."

"Well," said the homeless person, "that reminds me of a story!"

Oh NO...... Henry closed his eyes again, and considered his options. He could tell the man to shut up, there was always that. But then he'd have to listen to "Just because I'm *homeless* you think you got a right to treat me like an *animal!*" He could pretend he was really asleep, sound asleep, but then the guy would start pulling on him and jabbing him in the ribs. Neither of those outcomes appealed to him. He settled on a long sigh, heavy with the misery of the ages, and surrendered to his fate. It fit, after all. He was leaving this life because there was no peace; this was just more of the same. It proved him right.

The homeless person started talking then, in a deep voice that was easy on the ears:

"Once there was a bear that lived in a brokendown zoo in miserable conditions. It could go four paces in one direction, and four paces in another, or it could stay in one place and grumble; that was all the choices it had, year after year after year.

"The bear suffered greatly. And then the time came when the zoo changed hands, and a new and kinder

CHAPTER ONE

person was put in charge. The new keeper made the bear's cage many times larger, with rocks to climb on and a pool to swim in, and deep wide moats instead of bars. But still the bear went just four paces in one direction and four paces in another, or it stayed in one place and it grumbled. Because it wasn't paying attention. It didn't even notice that it had new choices, and it went right on suffering greatly."

There was a silence.
"That's *it*?" Henry snapped.
"That's it. Yes."
"Well, I've heard that story before, you know, and you've got it all wrong! In the *real* story, the bear is *blind!*"

The homeless person nodded. "That's right," he said. "And that's the point. The blind bear has an excuse; you *don't*."

Henry straightened up in the seat and looked at the man. He heard himself make a sharp noise of disbelief. Who did this raggedy dreg of humanity think he *was*, anyway?

"*Listen*, buddy!" he began. "You—"

But the man cut him off. "No. Please:*You* listen! Because it's very important. You have to pay *attention*.. To the world outside you, and the world within. You have to listen, and you have to observe. Otherwise, things will change and you won't even know. This is the first thing, the one that has to come before all the others. Nothing else can happen until you honor this First Rule."

"What?" Henry asked, befuddled now; he'd lost track. "This first *what*?"

The homeless person laid one hand gently on Henry's arm and leaned toward him. Henry hated that. The homeless were dirty, they were covered with germs, you could catch who knows what. He pulled away, hard.

"The First Rule," the man answered, letting go of Henry's arm and folding his hands in his lap. "The First Rule is: **PAY ATTENTION!**"

PEACETALK 101

Henry rolled his eyes, a woman behind them said, "Well you don't have to *yell!*", and he was glad that his stop was next.

"I'm getting off!" he said through clenched teeth, standing up and shoving past the homeless person.

When he got home he walked straight into the kitchen and told his wife, "I had to ride home this afternoon with a *crazy* man in the seat next to me!" He knew what she'd say back. She'd say, "Well, if you'd fix the *car*, Henry, you wouldn't *have* to ride the bus!", and he'd answer her with, "If you'd get a job and help *out*, Elizabeth, I'd have enough *money* to fix the car!" He knew what she'd say then, too; she'd say, "Well, if you'd *work* a little harder, Henry, I wouldn't *have* to get a job!" He got ready for all that.

But he was looking at her, and he noticed that the expression on her face wasn't right for that script, and he stopped.

"What did you say, Elizabeth?" he asked her.

"I said I'm sorry there's not enough money to get the car fixed."

Henry's mouth closed, and he stared at her. She looked tired, and she looked like she was a little bit afraid of him. How long, he wondered, had she been looking at him that way? He didn't know, he realized; he had no idea.

And then he remembered suddenly that she had good reason to be afraid of him, although she didn't know what he was planning.

"That's okay," he said carefully, looking down at the floor so he wouldn't have to see her eyes, wondering where she had put the child.

"It's okay, Elizabeth," he told the kitchen floor.

Henry tossed and turned that night. Miserable as he was, weary as he was, he couldn't get to sleep. It was like somebody had popped a tape recorder into his skull and set it to play the same stupid tape over and over and over. The tape said: *Listen, a man that's only got fourteen days*

CHAPTER ONE

of his life left, and the first one almost over, has got to DO SOMEthing! Henry would think *Do what?* **What?** — and it would answer him with *If you weren't such a **loser,** Henry, you'd **know**.* And Henry would think: *Know what?* **What?**

Just before midnight, just when he was sure he was going to lose his mind if it didn't stop, a thought came to him. All of a sudden, he knew what he could do. It wasn't much, but it was better than nothing. He slipped out of bed and went through the dark house to the closet by the front door, where he was sure he would be able to find what he needed.

Elizabeth wasn't a stingy woman, but she was careful with money. She always bought holiday stuff the day afterward, when it was all on sale, and she stored it in a big cardboard box on the front closet shelf until the holiday came round again. Henry pulled the box down, carried it into the kitchen, and set it on the table, where he could see well enough by the dim light over the stove.

The box was full of the usual junk. Wrapping paper and ribbon.... greeting cards.... silly paper hats, folded up. A tacky plastic globe that snowed when you turned it upside down. Just junk. Henry pawed through it — no need to be careful with it, since Elizabeth wasn't going to be here for any more holidays anyway, hoping. *Come on, Elizabeth,* he thought, *don't let me down this time!*

And there it was. One package of paper Advent calendars, as ordered, in a dirty plastic wrapper, marked down in the after-Christmas clearance sales to $3.45 for all three. Henry only needed one.

He took the calendar out of the wrapper and tore it carefully in half so there'd be exactly fourteen windows. There were five minutes left of the first day; he had time. Carefully, he took the little paper square that covered the first window between his fingers and pulled it back, to mark Day One.

He had been feeling almost sleepy, but when he saw what was framed in the little window he sat up straight and swore, and he was wide awake again. It was a bear. *A big white bear, like they keep in zoos.* The hairs on the back of his neck were rising — he could feel them — and he shuddered. And then he was disgusted with himself. It was a coincidence, that's all; it didn't mean anything. The tape recorder in his head agreed with him. *Sensible people don't pay attention to stuff like that, Henry,* it said.

The plastic mug on the kitchen table had a couple of pencils in it, for grocery lists; Henry reached over and grabbed one. Carefully again, with the seriousness the task deserved, he went back and forth over the bear with the pencil until the animal was hidden and there was nothing in the window any more but the kind of empty dull gray that he knew he'd see when he woke up tomorrow.

It was one minute past midnight; now, maybe, he could sleep. He put the calendar in his briefcase so he wouldn't forget to keep it with him, he put Elizabeth's box of holiday stash back in the closet, and he walked back through the shadows to his bed.

CHAPTER TWO

Henry woke up tired the next morning, thinking, as his eyes opened, "Here we go again — and I can't *face* it!"

But he knew better; he got up anyway.

He could hear a kind of mumbling noise that would be Elizabeth and the child eating breakfast, not waiting for him. That made sense, because he couldn't remember when he'd last eaten breakfast with them; still, he would have liked it a lot if they'd been waiting, or had at least called to him. If Elizabeth's voice had come sort of caroling through the air, going, "Honey? Your breakfast is ready!"

You're a nut case, Henry, he told himself scornfully, *a real nut case! Why should she do that?* He never talked to her, because he couldn't think of anything to say. He almost never touched her, because it seemed to him that he didn't really know her that well any more — and besides, he was so tired. Still....he had his ideas about how a wife ought to do things.

He figured it was a good thing he couldn't hear what they were saying, and one quick sideways look at them when he got to the kitchen was enough to make him sure he was right, so he just walked right through the kitchen past them and on out the door without even saying goodby.

He knew what he'd get back if he told her goodby, and

he couldn't face that either. Elizabeth would ask him whether he thought he'd be able to find the house when he came home, because the grass in the yard was knee-high and getting higher every day. And what could he say back? *Damned if I'll get out there in that heat and push a lawnmower, Elizabeth, just so the yard will look good when they find us dead?*?

No. He wasn't a mean man, and he was *not* going to say anything like that.

When he got to his bus stop, two women were there ahead of him. One was blonde, one redheaded, and from the way they were going at each other, he knew they had to be sisters.

The blonde said, "Listen, *I'm* the one that *bought* it! It was a dollar fifty-nine exactly!"

The redhead shot back with "It was a dollar sixty-*four*, stupid!"

"A dollar fifty-*nine*, I tell you!"

"*Sixty-four!*"

"*Fifty-nine!*"

"**Sixty-four!**"

Five cents; and they were willing to ruin the whole morning over it. Sadness slid down over Henry, gray and soggy as a sweatshirt left out in the rain. He dug in his pocket, found two nickels, and offered each of them one.

"Here," he said. "Let me help! Have a nickel!"

The women drew away from him as if he might be some kind of crazed killer. They hissed at him about people who can't mind their own business, and went on with their argument in shrill whispers, with their backs turned to him.

Not until the bus was in sight did it occur to Henry that in fact he *was* a killer, in a way. That the women were *right* to look at him like that. In a way. It gave him a funny feeling. It made him burn inside with anger at the women, because until then he hadn't thought of himself as a killer.

CHAPTER TWO

Not once. They had made it happen, them and their nickel. *This,* he thought wonderingly, *must be what causes 'random' killings. Somebody like me runs into somebody like them, somebody says something, somebody says something back.* And then it all goes terribly wrong in a way that you could never, never explain. It would be *their* fault. The way the idea he now had of himself as a killer was their fault.

Still, the women got the last two seats on the bus, and Henry had to stand. He stood there, holding his briefcase with one hand and the overhead bar with the other, thinking how there's no justice, while more people shoehorned on at every stop and everybody who was already on yelled at the driver to *keep on going for gods sake couldn't he tell the bus was FULL?* And then he looked up and found himself wedged tight against the homeless lunatic he'd had for seatmate the night before.

He said it out loud, then, and he didn't try to keep his voice down: "There's NO JUStice!"

"Right on, buddy!" yelled the people on the bus, like a choir. And "You got that right!" And one voice went, "Somebody hand me a string for these pearls of wisdom, willya?"

"Do you really believe that?" The homeless person was asking him that, right in his face. "You really believe there's no justice?" The guy even looked interested. People like him would do anything to get you involved.

"Damn *right* I believe it!" Henry snapped.

"Well," said the homeless person, "that reminds me of a story."

If Henry had had the means, he might have given up the rest of his thirteen days and killed himself right then and there. Even though it would have meant failing in his duty to his wife and to the child, leaving them behind and all alone in a world that he knew would only neglect and abuse them. At that instant, with the rage and despair swirling through him, it seemed to him that it would have made perfectly good sense. But he was trapped; he didn't even have a free hand.

The homeless person said:

"Once there was a lawyer who got up one morning and looked out at the sky and saw that it looked exactly like dryer lint. The lawyer was—"

"*What?!*" Henry interrupted. "Now *wait* a minute! There's no such *thing* as a story that talks about dryer lint!"

The homeless man ignored him and went right on....

"The lawyer was an educated man; he knew what that sky meant. It meant that it was going to rain. And so he went out on his front steps, opened his umbrella over his head, and walked off toward his office. He got there without a single drop of rain falling on him. And so did everybody else — even though they weren't carrying umbrellas."

There was a long silence; the homeless man looked straight into Henry's eyes.

"That's it?' Henry demanded. "That's *all?*"

"Isn't it enough?"

"No!" Henry said. "What kind of fool excuse for a story is *that* supposed to be?"

"You have a point," said the homeless man. "Here, let me try again." And he said...

"Once there was a little girl from a minimum-wage family who really wanted to do something to help her parents out, and so she decided she'd keep a garden. There was no yard around the old apartment building where they lived. But there was a flat roof, and there was a pile of dirt out by the alley; she thought she could probably manage. She decided to grow roses, because that would cheer her mother up, and potatoes, because

CHAPTER TWO

her father loved them fried. She took two cardboard boxes up to the roof, and carried up paper bags of dirt until she had the boxes filled up, and she stuck a rose in one and a cut-up potato in the other.

"When her parents asked her what she was doing, she told them; she was an honest child. Her mother looked at her sadly and shook her head, and said "*You* can't grow anything on the *roof* in a cardboard *box! That's riDICulous!*" And her father rolled his eyes and said it was so dumb he couldn't believe he'd heard her say it, it was the dumbest idea he'd ever HEARD.

"So the little girl didn't water the boxes of dirt. The rose turned brown in its box and fell over dead, and the potatoes rotted in their box and drew flies. And the mother and father said, "*See?* We *told* you you couldn't do it! Let that be a *lesson* to you!" And it was; and the child learned it well."

Henry jumped when it was over, he'd been listening so hard. Why, he didn't know; maybe because he'd kept thinking that surely there was going to be a punch line sometime.

"*Awwwwwwwwwwwwwwwww!*" It came out of his mouth; he wasn't sure what it was, only that it carried his outrage.

"What's the matter?"

"THAT'S not a story!"

"Well," said the man, looking off to one side, "you didn't want to hear a story anyway."

That was true, but Henry didn't like hearing it; he was sure he hadn't actually said it. "I suppose you can read my mind," he sneered.

"I don't *have* to read your mind. Because I'm paying attention, I can read your face and your shoulders and your arms and legs ... all the parts of your body. They were all saying you didn't want to hear a story."

"Well then, why did you decide to go ahead and *tell* one?"

The homeless man smiled at him. "I didn't," he said. "You said so yourself. Both times."

Henry swallowed hard. He didn't know how he'd gotten into this and he didn't know how to get out.

"And that," said the homeless person, "brings me to the rule. The Second Rule is: **REJECT PRECONCEPTIONS**."

"Preconwhat?" said somebody across the aisle; and somebody else said, "*Preconceptions*, dummy! Means don't leap to conclusions in ad*vance*. Have an open *mind*. Stuff like that!"

Henry drew his eyebrows together and narrowed his eyes in the fiercest face he knew how to make. He leaned closer to the homeless man, never mind the germs, and through clenched teeth he said, "*You* had better not be *next* to me on this bus when I go home tonight! I'm WARNing you!"

Behind him a woman said, "Well, you don't have to YELL!"

That night, the homeless person wasn't on the bus when Henry got on, and the bus wasn't crowded; he had a whole seat to himself. *Which just goes to show*, he told himself, *that if you stick up for your rights you can sometimes come out the winner.* He leaned back in the seat, enjoying the quiet in spite of the way the diesel fuel stank in the heavy summer air.

It was a good time for tidying things up, with nobody to bother him. He straightened some papers in his briefcase, and scribbled a note he'd been meaning to write. And then he took out the Advent calendar and a pencil, to cross off the second day in the rest of his life. He opened the second little window, in its frame of faded silver glitter, and looked inside.

And there in the window was a small girl, holding a rose.

"AHAH!" Henry said softly, but ferociously. "Where's your potato?" And then again, "Yeah, kid, where's your poTAto?"

CHAPTER TWO

Slowly, enjoying every second of it, he took his pencil and he covered the little girl up. He made her and her sappy rose disappear. He buried them under a perfectly seamless and satiny layer of dark gray pencil lead, until the second window was just as blank as the first one. There'd been a little girl, sure, and a rose. But no potato. Just like the bear, it was a coincidence, and it wasn't even a very *good* coincidence.

For the first time in many months, Henry felt almost cheerful. *Maybe I should pay attention to the feeling,* he thought. *It may be my last chance.*

PEACETALK 101

CHAPTER THREE

Henry woke up the next day with a vague idea that something had happened the day before, something he'd meant to remember. On his way out he stopped at the breakfast table and asked his wife a question.

"Elizabeth, when I got home yesterday did I tell you to remind me of anything this morning?"

She looked up at him and smiled, shaking her head. "No," she said. And then: "Henry, why don't you sit down and have some breakfast with us?"

Henry frowned at her. "Aren't you going to ask me why I haven't mowed the grass?"

"No," she said. "Aren't you going to ask me why I haven't cleaned the refrigerator?"

"You haven't done that *yet*?"

"No," said Elizabeth.

"Well, it doesn't matter," he said, and went on out the door, wondering what it was that he'd forgotten. Behind him, he could hear Elizabeth calling after him, but he knew it couldn't be anything important; he didn't stop to check it out.

The quarreling sisters weren't at his bus stop this time, which was a relief. Maybe they'd just been passing through. The crazy homeless person who apparently considered this bus his domain did turn up — but the empty seat beside him wasn't the last one; there was another empty in the row just ahead. That was a relief, too. That made two good things happening in a single morning, he realized — three, if he counted not getting chewed out about the grass.

Brace yourself, Henry! he thought as he took the other empty seat. *Whatever's coming next is going to be a real downer!* And so he wasn't surprised when the homeless man leaned forward and laid a hand on his shoulder and said "Good morning!"

Henry jerked his shoulder away and stared straight ahead. Maybe if he just ignored the man he'd give up and go bother somebody else.

"You know," said the homeless man, "that reminds me of a story."

See? Henry flung the silent question at the universe. *You see what I mean? There is no PEACE! I'm like a bug pinned on a piece of cardboard here!*

But the universe said nothing back, and the homeless man went right on talking.

"Once there was a rooster with a scientific turn of mind who decided to carry out a research project. He went from animal to animal, all around the barnyard, paying very close attention to what happened, listening carefully, and rejecting all preconceptions. To each one in turn — the goat, the pig, the cow, the horse, the donkey, the cat, the turkey, and the dog — he put the same question: "Tell me, can you talk?" He spoke clearly and carefully, and he spoke loudly enough to be absolutely sure that he was heard. But not a single animal answered his question.

"When he had made his way back once more to the chicken coop, he reported his results to the hens. 'We now know,' he told them, 'that the chicken is the only animal that speaks a language; I've proved it.' And the hens set up a great clamor of admiration and told him how proud of him they all were.

"Meanwhile, the goats, the pigs, the cows, the horses,

CHAPTER THREE

the donkeys, the cats, the turkeys, and the dogs were discussing the morning's events with their mates and relatives. And they were saying what a shame it was that a creature as handsome and energetic as the rooster had no language and could only make meaningless noises.

"And that brings us to the Third Rule, which is: STAY IN TUNE."

The woman sitting next to Henry in the seat by the window turned her head and spoke to him. "I don't get it," she said. "Do you get it?"

Henry shrugged. "You think that one's bad, you should have heard the *last* one he told! All about a rose and a potato."

"You're kidding!"

"No," said Henry, "it's the truth."

The woman did something Henry never would have done, because he had better sense. She turned around in her seat and asked the homeless person behind them to explain.

"What's staying in *tune* got to do with anything?" she challenged him. "I thought the story was about chickens!"

"If you sing in the key of C and the person you're with sings in the key of G, there can't be any music," said the homeless man.

"Like she said," Henry put in. "Chickens, buddy, chickens!"

"If you're talking French," said the homeless man, "and the person you're with is talking Cherokee, there can't be any conversation."

There was a long silence, and then Henry got ready to tell the guy off. He was going to say that even a homeless person ought to know that when somebody says something to you, what you say back is supposed to have some kind of connection to what came before! But the woman beside him cut him off.

"Shhh!" she said. "Hush! I think I'm beginning to get it!"

Beginning to get it?

Henry couldn't believe his ears. He wanted to take her by the shoulders and shake some sense into her. Because that would have gotten him arrested, he settled for just talking forcefully to her.

"LISten," he said, "you are NOT 'beginning to get it'! There nothing to GET, don't you KNOW THAT? There's nothing...."

"WELL!" the woman said, interrupting him again. "You DON'T have to YELL!"

When Henry got to his office, still seething, the man who had the desk next to his said "Good morning!", without looking up.

"What's *good* about it?" Henry snarled

"Well, excuse *me!*" said the other man. "Just trying to be polite."

"I have spent the *last two hours,*" Henry said, spitting out each word like a bullet, "in one insane conversation after *anoth*er! It's a MADhouse out there! So don't YOU start!"

His colleague looked up at him then, and looked him up and down in silence. And then he spoke in a flat and chilly voice. "Hey .... if I was on fire, I wouldn't open my mouth to YOU again, Henry — you can COUNT on it!" And he got up and stalked out, leaving Henry alone in the little room, staring after him.

Henry wondered if there was any point in trying to go after him and explain, and thought about the wild tale he'd have to tell if he did. *In another twelve days I'll just be history to the guy anyway,* he thought, and gave it up. He sat down at his desk behind the pile of boring work he'd have to do that day, and tried to pull himself together.

It was only nine o'clock, but it seemed to him that he'd already been through a whole day's worth of hassle. He might just as well open the third window and mark this day off, because it sure wasn't going to get any better; it

CHAPTER THREE

might as well be over. He wished it *were* over, then he would already have finished with those stacks of files and papers.

He took the Advent calendar out of his briefcase and smoothed it out on the top of his desk. The first two windows looked blindly back at him, both made empty by his trusty pencil. He looked at the third window, still closed, and said softly, "This one is going to be a candy cane. Or a stupid star." He took the little flap between his fingers and pulled it back.

And there it was, framed in glitter, looking right at him. *A rooster.*

Henry closed the window again, and laid his hands flat over the surface of the calendar; it didn't quite hide the whole thing away, but it hid most of it.

Get a grip, Henry! he thought. He was acting like some kind of superstitious old biddy, instead of like what he was, an educated person who knew about probability. It had to stop.

He took his hands away from the calendar, folded them in his lap, and lectured himself. *Every time you toss a coin, every single time, it's just as likely to be heads or tails as it was the time before. You start over every time — the odds don't change. You can get heads ten times in a row ... a hundred times in a row.... the odds are always exactly the same!*

It was true. It was something he knew and understood, and he was ashamed of himself for letting a string of coincidences — *remember the potato!* — shake him up.

Henry picked up his pencil. With a steady hand, he made the third window look just like the other two. Empty; blank; and gray.

PEACETALK 101

CHAPTER FOUR

"Elizabeth," Henry said, pausing at the kitchen table on his way out, "I may be late tonight — I've got a meeting."

"Okay," she said, "I'll fix something that can wait." And then: "Why don't you sit down and have some breakfast with us?"

Same thing she tried yesterday, he thought. *What's she up to?*

"If it wasn't for the meeting," he said, "I might mow the front yard."

"Henry?"

"Yes?"

"Please, Henry — please pay attention."

He had already turned his back on her, but that line stopped him; he turned around with his hand on the door, and waited.

"Henry," she said, "I asked you: Why don't you sit down and have some breakfast with Timmy and me?"

Yesterday's version of this episode came back into his mind then — what she'd said, what he'd said — and it played in his head like a movie. She had asked him that yesterday. "Why don't you sit down and have some breakfast with us?' And he had said back: "Aren't you going to ask me why I haven't mowed the grass?"

When somebody says something to you, what you say back is supposed to have some kind of connection to what came before.

Henry cleared his throat. "Yeah, why don't I?" he said. It was the best he could do. He was almost ready to sit down in his chair when she spoke again.

"We've got fried potatoes," she said. "The kind you really like."

Henry sat down carefully. "No potatoes," he said. "Just toast."

The day was long, and the meeting seemed longer than the day; by the time he climbed on the bus it was getting dark outside and he was worn out. *Only eleven days to go,* he told himself sternly. *And this one's almost over. You can do **anything** for just eleven days!* The part of him that came bleating back about being too tired to do even one more day disgusted him, because in this world a man does whatever he has to do; he ignored it and looked around him, hoping for a window seat.

No problem; the bus was nearly empty. Not many people rode out to the tacky suburb where Henry lived, once rush hour was over. He had his choice of a dozen window seats. Having any kind of choice was such a treat that he took his time. Did he want to sit in the back where the bus cleaning crews always ran out of energy and left most of the dirt undisturbed? Did he want to sit up toward the front, where it was a lot cleaner but you had to eat diesel fumes every time the bus stopped? Henry turned it over and over in his mind like a man trying to decide between steak and lobster.

A voice came at him then from the very back seat, where the light was so dim that Henry hadn't been able to see who was sitting there. A rich deep voice that was easy on the ears.

"Why don't you come on back here and sit with me?" the homeless person asked.

He rides the bus at night, too??

The word that came immediately to Henry's mind was one Elizabeth strongly objected to hearing him say; he swallowed that word and said one only slightly milder.

CHAPTER FOUR

"You watch your mouth on my bus!" the driver snapped.

"Does it really matter?" he asked her wearily. "It's not a gun, you know, it's just a word."

"*You* heard me!" she said. "Don't you give me 'only a word'! Just watch your mouth!"

If she was going to be like that, he was going to get as far from her as he could. He went all the way back to the back and sat down in the dark corner opposite to the corner where the homeless man was lurking, leaned back against the dirty upholstery, and closed his eyes.

"That," the homeless man began, "reminds me of a—"

"Wait!" Henry said. He opened his eyes and sat up straight. "You wait! Just hold on a minute! Don't you think you ought to get off this bus once in a while and get yourself a *life*? Doesn't it ever occur to you that you're *bothering people*?"

"That's a preconception, friend."

"*What's* a preconception? And I'm not your friend."

"It's a preconception, deciding 'Oh, I won't tell people any stories — they don't want to hear them. All these tired, bored, worried, lonesome, miserable people...they won't want to hear a story.' That's a preconception. And it's a terrific excuse for not doing anything, too."

"But what if they really *don't* want to hear it?"

"Then they should say so. Expecting other people to read your mind and know what you want and don't want isn't rational."

This homeless loony is telling me what's rational! Henry thought. It was unbelievable!

"I'm going to say something rational now," he said. "Get ready!"

"Go for it!"

"I don't want to hear a story — it would bother me."

"Good enough," said the homeless man.

"And I don't want to hear one of your phony stories

that doesn't have a point, either, so don't try that."

"A story that has no point cannot be recognized as a story," said the homeless man.

"And I suppose that's the Fourth Rule!" Harry said crossly.

"No. It's not."

"Well, what *is?*"

The homeless man started moving toward Henry's side of the bus, but when Henry held up a warning hand, he sighed and moved back into the corner.

"Well?" Henry said.

"It doesn't work that way."

"Doesn't work *what* way? Can't you talk sense?"

"People who want to know what the Rules are have two choices: They can either listen to the stories that go with the Rules, or they can figure the Rules out for themselves."

Henry gritted his teeth and said nothing, and the bus rolled on through the dark. But the driver had different ideas.

"You back there," she said. "I *do* want to know what the Fourth Rule is. And I'm willing to sit through a story to find out."

"You're just *encouraging* him to bother people!" Henry yelled.

"Watch your mouth, mister," the driver said calmly. "And pay attention. The man's gonna tell us a story."

It never stopped! It never, never let up, not even for a minute!

Henry closed his eyes, whipped again, and the homeless man began...

"Once there was a turtle with a bad attitude. People would go down to the muddy river and stick their feet in the water to cool off, and the turtle would bite the ends of their toes off. That taught the people to stay dry. But it didn't stop there. The turtle would wait in the shallows, and when people walked by or sat down at the edge of the

CHAPTER FOUR

water to relax for a minute he'd reach his long mean neck right up out of the water and bite them. And he wouldn't let go till it suited him, either. He was a menace and a hazard, and he ruined the river for everybody. The people decided they had to catch the turtle and get rid of him so the river would belong to everybody once again instead of to the turtle. And they tried hard. They tried everything they could think of. They started out baiting their lines with worms and crickets and minnows; when the turtle paid no attention, they tried small fish, both dead ones and live ones, and they tried frogs, both big ones and little ones. The turtle would have nothing to do with any of it.

"And then one day a little boy said to the grownups, 'I think I know how to get that turtle to bite.'

"'You do?' said the grownups.

"'I think he wants something good,' said the little boy. 'Not worms and stuff, something good. Like... like a garlic salami.'"

Henry jumped. "LISten, you!" he began. "You—" But the driver hit the horn and startled him quiet.

"Don't interrupt!" she yelled. "It's RUDE!" And then, "Go on, you back there."

"So they put a garlic salami on the line and the turtle could not resist. The way it smelled was like an enchantment to him. He swam around it for almost a minute, trying to think of a way to get it off the line without actually taking it in his mouth, but he was only a turtle; he couldn't think of any way to do it. He knew what was going to happen to him if he took it. He told his turtle self, *You know what's going to happen to you if you bite on that thing! Don't DO it!* But he couldn't stand it. It was so tempting It was so tantalizing. He just could not let it go by. He took a giant bite, and he felt the hook set in his long mean neck, and that was the last thing he felt before the people chopped his head off, salami and all."

"Rule Four," the homeless man added in the silence, "is: **TAKE NO BAIT.**"

Henry got off the bus, muttering to himself, and walked home. *Pay attention. Reject preconceptions. Stay in tune. Take no bait.* It all ran through his head; it seemed to him that he could feel his brain flinching away from it, trying to get out of the way. *What was the guy getting at, anyway?* **Two** *could play that game! First rule:* **Turn blue.** *Second rule:* **Drop dead.** *Third rule:* **Outa my face!** *Fourth rule:* **Watch your mouth**. That one he owed to the bus driver; he'd give her credit for it.

"Next time I see that turkey," he said aloud as he turned up his front walk, "I'll give him *my* rules! We'll see how he likes *that!*"

When Elizabeth and the child were in bed, he went to the kitchen table to open the next window on the Advent calendar. He knew he should just throw it away. He should just wad it up and throw it in the trash and be done with it. It was nothing but a stupid piece of paper, and it wasn't accomplishing one thing except to irritate him. But he couldn't stand it. He had to know what was behind that window. Because it couldn't be a turtle, could it?

How could it be a turtle?

It couldn't be a turtle, because the calendar was a Christmas thing. And turtles are maybe a Fourth of July thing, but not Christmas.

It was a turtle.

Henry could have kicked himself. If he'd just had backbone enough to throw the calendar away, he would have been all right. He would not have had to know that what appeared in Window Four was a turtle, with a cursed bow tied around its cursed neck!

You don't learn, Henry, he told himself bitterly as he lay down beside Elizabeth, so tired that he ached all over. *You just don't learn....*

CHAPTER FIVE

The time was coming when he would have to start *doing* things, Henry realized. The days were going by.

For himself, it was easy: just pills, a strong rubber band, and a garbage bag. He'd been worried that he might have to go to Mexico or someplace for the pills, but it turned out that you just go stand in an alley in a bad neighborhood and wave some cash. Twitchy kids would come and take your order, like it was a fast food place.

The problem was Elizabeth and the child. As usual. It would take whole handfuls of pills, and there was no way to get all that into somebody unless they were cooperating. Guns and knives were out because he was a coward. Putting them in the car and shoving it off a cliff was out because he was a wimp. The whole *point* was for them never to know what was happening. He loved them, or at least he could *remember* loving them; he couldn't stand the thought of them knowing.

He had figured out how to do it, finally, lying on his bed in the long empty nights, his mind humming along, tormenting him. A couple of pills to knock them out — he could manage that — and a rag stuffed in the exhaust pipe of the car. He'd tuck them in and turn on the engine, and they'd just sleep till it was all over. And then, once he knew they were safe, *once he knew that nothing could ever hurt either one of them again,* he'd go in the house and do his thing with the pills and the bag.

But to do that he had to get the car fixed. You can't send somebody out of this world on the carbon monoxide trip if you can't start your car. So when Elizabeth asked him to have some breakfast again, he said, "I can't, I have to see about getting the car fixed."

It was true. He had to go in early so he could get the parts Ralph said he needed, and he had to go by Ralph's shop and talk him into coming over and doing the work.

He had Ralph and the car on his mind when he got on the bus; it wasn't until the homeless man sat down that it came to him that he wasn't going to have to put up with this longwinded pain in the neck much longer. Because that made him feel almost friendly, he answered the guy's "Good morning!" with "Same to you." And then he had a thought.

"Hey!" he said. "I've got a question. How many of those rules have you got? I mean the ones that go with your dumb stories. How many of them are there?"

The man smiled. "Twelve," he said. "Just twelve."

"Well, I won't have to listen to all of them," Henry said, with great satisfaction. "I'm getting my car fixed, so I won't have to keep taking the bus. So your plan isn't going to work — you're going to have to start all over, buddy, with some other pigeon!"

The homeless man sighed a long heavy sigh and said, "That's sad news. I'm sorry to hear it."

"So you might as well not waste your time with me today," Henry went on. 'You might as well go look for your next victim. Okay?"

"That's sad news. I'm sorry to hear it."

Henry decided to try an experiment. He said, "And Mary had a little lamb, its fleece was white as snow."

"That's sad news. I'm sorry to hear it," said the homeless man.

Henry stared at him. "Are you just going to keep on saying that, over and over?" he asked.

CHAPTER FIVE

"Only until you listen to it, instead of just hearing it."

Henry rubbed his chin and thought about that; there was something to it, he had to admit that. He shrugged his shoulders. "Okay," he said, "I'm game. Say it again, and this time I'll listen. I'll pay attention."

"That's sad news, about not getting to talk to you any more," said the homeless man. "I'm sorry to hear it."

Henry was amazed. "You *mean* that," he said slowly. "You really mean what you're *say*ing!"

"You've got it. Sure I do."

"But *why?*"

The homeless man smiled again. "Let me answer that with a story," he said.

"Now wait a minute! That's not *fair!* You can't—"

The homeless man cut him off. "It's a really short one," he said. "It won't take but a minute." He added, "I'm sorry I interrupted you," and then...

"Once there was a little boy who loved his father very much and wanted to please him. He knew his dad was crazy about dogs — epecially Irish setters — and so he decided to paint an Irish setter for him. It could be a Father's Day present, the little boy thought. Or if he couldn't get it done that fast, it could be a birthday present.

"He didn't hurry, because it was important to do it right. First he found a good photograph of a setter and traced it, and practiced tracing it over and over until he felt like his hand had learned its lines. He knew of course that giving his dad a *traced* picture would be cheating; he had to learn to do it from scratch. When he thought he had it, he drew the dog on a sheet of heavy paper, and he mixed his colors and painted it, taking a long time over every detail. He held it up to the light and looked at it inside, and he took it outside and looked at it in the sunlight. He changed a thing or two that the light had helped him see. All in all, it took him a whole month, and Father's Day did go by before he was done.

"And then came his dad's birthday. The little boy

smoothed the picture out and wrapped it in shiny paper and tied on a blue-and-silver-striped ribbon and bow, and took it to his dad. He waited while the bow was untied and the paper was taken off; and he watched while the picture was held out at arm's length and studied.

"And then his father turned to him and said, 'Thank you, son. What *is* it?'"

It hit Henry right in the gut, that story. The time it happened to him, it had been his mother, and it was a potholder he'd made for her at school. Somebody behind him said, "Story of my life!" and somebody else agreed. The whole bus was listening. You could tell. You could feel the remembering going back and forth.

"Well?" Henry said, swallowing hard. "What's the rule?"

"Rule Five," said the homeless man. "**PRESERVE FACE**."

"Yeah!" said the driver, his voice loud in the silence. "Why make the little kid feel stupid? What's it cost the guy to just say thanks and it's really a nice picture, instead?"

Yeah! Henry thought. *How much could it cost, to do that instead?*

But a man sitting in the next row of seats turned around, shaking his head. "It's a *lie* to say that," he announced, like it was news. "What's more, you coddle a kid that way, the other kids'll have him for breakfast! You gotta make your kids *tough*, or their lives are gonna...be...*hell*."

"Right," said Henry, lying, "exactly what I was thinking."

"You got kids?" the man asked him.

"One," Henry said. "Just one.

"A case like that, you'd do the right thing, right? You'd tell the kid, straight up, you can't even tell what it's supposed to be a picture *of!* Am I right? And if he started blubbering, you'd tell him to straighten up and act like a *man*, right?"

CHAPTER FIVE

You don't blubber, Henry thought. *You don't cry. You don't say* **one word.** *You just go on away so you can be by yourself, and you feel like a great big sharp rock is stuck in your chest.*

"There's something you can say," the homeless man told them, "something that's true, and isn't coddling the child."

"Oh, yeah?" Henry and the man ahead of him said it together, like they'd been practicing.

"Yeah. You don't say 'Thank you — what is it?' You say 'I can tell you really worked hard on this picture, and I thank you very much for painting it for me.' That's not a lie... and nobody loses face."

When Henry got to his office, the man who had the desk next to him was already there. It occurred to Henry that he might tell him he was sorry he'd taken his head off the other day. He could say, "Sorry about that; I was just having a bad day." But he knew what would happen — the guy would give him that icy look, and make some smart crack, and he'd feel like a fool.

That's a preconception.

He could hear it in his head. He ignored it, because it wasn't the only thing he could hear in his head. He could also hear his mother, while she kept turning the pathetic potholder around and around in her hands, saying "What *is* it, dear? What *is* it, Henry?" He sat down and pulled a stack of file folders over in front of him, slapped one open, and went to work. He had to get it all done, so he could leave early enough to go buy those parts and talk to Ralph about the car.

When he opened the fifth window that night, he had a different attitude. In advance, he told himself: *"It may be a present this time. A gift. So what? There's always one window that's got a present in it! It doesn't mean anything.*

When he saw the little gift box, and the silver-and-blue-striped ribbon and bow on it, he didn't even blink. He didn't let it get to him at all. It didn't mean a thing. He just took his pencil and covered it over with broad lines of gray until it was gone, just like he had with all the others.

It didn't mean a thing.

CHAPTER SIX

"UH-oh!"

Ralph was bent over the car's engine, humming his personal version of "Summertime," while Henry watched.

"What?" Henry asked, thinking that there's no such thing as a mechanic that can't find something else wrong besides what you call him for, even when the mechanic is a friend. "What's the matter?"

"Henry," said Ralph from under the hood, "you got the wrong part, man!"

"I got what you *told* me to get!"

"Then somebody *gave* you the wrong part. Either way, it won't work."

Henry sighed. Naturally. You get to the weekend, you're looking forward to taking it easy, and something screws it up. Always! *There is NO PEACE, ever!*

"So what do we do?" he asked Ralph warily.

"What *I* do is, I have a beer, and then I start working on the stuff you got the right parts for. What *you* do is you get on the bus and go exchange this thing for what you were supposed to get." He reached in his jeans pocket and pulled out a pencil and a scrap of paper. "Here," he said, straightening up. "I'll write it down. You take this thing back and you show them this piece of paper — see here, where I wrote it out? Part number, part description, et cetera? Tell them that's what you need.

And then you come on back and we'll finish 'er up."

"How about if I take your truck, Ralph?" It was worth a try.

Ralph shook his head. "I'm sorry, buddy," he said, "but I can't let you do that. If I get a call..." He tapped the phone on his belt. "I may have to go do a tow. I told you that, yesterday. Remember?"

Henry remembered. "Sure," he said. "Sure. Okay."

"Here." Ralph handed him the note, and the part that wouldn't work. "The bus isn't so bad," he said. "I ride it myself sometimes, so I don't have to worry about parking."

"It's not the bus I object to," Henry said. "It's the loony riding it with me."

"What loony?"

"Oh, some homeless guy. He's decided I'm the boat and he's the barnacle. Every time I take the bus, there he is, right in my face. Likes to tell me stories. *Stupid* stories."

Ralph took a beer from the sixpack on the floor. "Big burly guy?" he asked Henry. "Black hair with a white streak in front? Kind of a grungy grizzly beard? Wears green sweats?"

"I never noticed what he looked like, Ralph, or what he was wearing. He's driving me *nuts,* that's all *I* know about him!"

"Yeah? That doesn't sound like Joe. He always backs off right away if you tell him to. Joe's a nice guy. He rides the bus, he pays his fare, he tells stories, he helps little old ladies with their packages and does *not* hit 'em up for money, after — he's okay. Must be your loony's somebody else."

Henry shrugged; he didn't know, and he didn't care.

"I'll be right back," he said, "quick as I can."

And he headed for the bus stop, thinking *Maybe I'll be lucky. Maybe Homeless-and-Clueless will be taking Saturday off.*

But the man was there. He had black hair with a white streak in the front, and a grungy grizzly beard; he was

CHAPTER SIX

wearing green sweats. The bus was full of screaming kids, women who all looked like they had splitting headaches, and Joe.

"Hey, Joe," Henry said, sitting down beside him; it was either sit by Joe or sit by one of the screaming kids.

"Good morning," said the homeless man. "You have to work Saturdays?"

"Naah. I'm just going to town to get something and bring it back."

"Like a great explorer going after undiscovered treasures."

"No. Like a donkey going after firewood."

"That's how you see it, huh?"

"Hey, that's how it *is*," Henry said bitterly. "That's what life is like. Haul the rock up the hill, so it can roll back down, so you can haul it back up again the next day. You mean you haven't noticed?"

"What's your rock?"

"My rock?"

"That's a metaphor," the homeless man said. "Like 'time is money,' and 'life is a bowl of cherries.' In the metaphor you've chosen, the world is a steep hill, and you haul the same rock up it, day after day, right? So — what's your rock?"

What's my rock? My life is my rock! Henry thought. The job, the wife, the child, the dog; the mother dwindling away, that doesn't even know who you are any longer; the Congressman, the father-in-law, the bickering and whining and needling and poking at you, the whole shebang. *My life is a gigantic boulder that I haul up the hill every day, on my bleeding back.*

"Hey, I didn't choose it!" he objected, without answering the question. It was nobody else's business, what his own personal rock was. "It's what got *laid* on me."

"There's that donkey again," said the homeless man.

Henry stared at him. "*Why* am I talking to you?' he asked suddenly. "Listen, will you tell your blasted story and get it over with, please? And keep it *short*."

"All right," said the homeless man, "Here we go — fast forward." And he began...

"Once there was a woman who woke up one day and discovered that there'd been a blizzard during the night and she was snowed in. She had no lights, no heat, no television; she couldn't use her computer or her blender or her microwave. Snow was everywhere; she couldn't get her car out, she couldn't even walk. She'd have had to wear skis to go anywhere! It was awful, and it went on for three days. When it was over at last, the woman sent an angry letter to the Governor chewing him out because he hadn't sent the National Guard to clear the roads and bring in the power trucks the very first day. 'We were in the middle of a *disaster*, and you let us do*wn!*' she wrote. 'I will never, *never*, vote for you again!'

"And then summer came, with the first long holiday weekend. The woman had been looking forward to it all year long. She packed up her gear and her tent and went camping. For three days she had no lights, no air conditioning, and no television. She couldn't use her computer or her blender or her microwave. She had such a wonderful time that she made reservations to do it again over the Fourth of July. In fact, she had such a wonderful time that she decided she'd do it again over Chistmas, and take her skis along so she could *really* enjoy it."

Henry sat silently, thinking about that.
"Was that short enough?" Joe asked him.
"Mmhmmm," Henry said; he was still thinking. "And the Sixth Rule is?"
"The Sixth Rule is: **CHOOSE YOUR METAPHORS**."
"I don't get it," Henry said.
"It'll come to you," said Joe, pleasantly. He clasped his hands behind his neck and leaned his head back on them and closed his eyes. "Just don't fight it," he said. "Just give it a chance."
When Henry got back home with the car part he found

CHAPTER SIX

Ralph busy under the hood, which was what he'd been hoping for. He also found the child sitting on a cardboard box beside Ralph talking a blue streak, and that was something else again.

"Hey, *you!*" he said to the child. "The man's trying to fix the car! You go on inside and stop bothering him!"

The child jumped off the box and ran into the house like a bear was after him.

"Why'd you do that?" Ralph demanded, taking the part out of Henry's hand.

"Do what?"

"Why'd you scare your kid like that? He wasn't doing anything wrong."

"I didn't 'scare' him, as you put it, I just told him to quit *bothering* you."

"He wasn't bothering me, Henry. We were having a conversation."

"A conversation? You and that child?"

"Henry," said Ralph, sounding cross, "pay attention! That child — as you put it — has a name. He tells me his name is Timmy. And he can talk just fine, Henry."

"He can?"

"Well, don't you *know, man?* What happens when *you* talk to him?"

Henry tried to think when he had last talked to the child. Correction: When he had last talked to Timmy. He couldn't remember.

"He's just a little tiny kid," he said sullenly. "He's just barely three."

"A three-year-old kid is a person, Henry, just like you and I are persons. A kid is not a pet, or a machine, or some kind of alien from outer space. A kid is a *person!*"

If that's true, Henry thought, *a kid is just somebody else that's going to try to boss me around and lie to me, and promise me things and then not do them, and make excuses, and throw smart cracks and nosy questions at me. I don't need that.*

Out loud, he said, "I'll have conversations with him

when he gets older and starts making sense!" Ralph had a lot of nerve, criticizing him for the way he treated Timmy! What did Ralph know about it, anyway? And then he remembered that one more thing Ralph didn't know was that Timmy wouldn't be getting a chance to get older and start making sense.

"Let's just fix the car, ol' buddy," he said quickly, staring off into space, "and never mind the child psychology! Okay?"

Ralph gave him a look that Henry didn't care for, and Henry clenched his jaw and gave it right back. Man to man, eye to eye, until the mechanic gave up and shrugged his shoulders.

"Okay, Henry," Ralph said. "It's your call."

I won, Henry told himself. *I won*. And the voice in his head, the one that was on the tapes, sneered at him: *SO?*

Henry opened Window Six that night after Elizabeth and Timmy went to bed. He saw the pair of skis framed in the tiny window, and he nodded his head. Okay. Okay! *Just keep it up,* he shouted silently toward the universe at large. *You just go right ahead! I'm not going to let it bother me in **any** way!*

And he took his pencil in his hand and made the skis disappear.

CHAPTER SEVEN

When Henry woke up the next morning it was Sunday, and the child... Timmy ...was on his mind. His first thought wasn't "Here-we-go-again-and-I-can't-*face*-it," it was "Timmy hasn't had time to do much of anything and there's not much time *left!*"

It was strange starting the day that way. It startled him. It made him feel like he'd waked up in somebody else's house. It struck him suddenly that the other thought had turned into a ritual for him. The way some people start their day with a prayer or a curse or one of those stupid "I'm getting *better!*" jingles, he had been saluting every dawn with "Here we go again — and I can't *face* it!" He turned over on his back and lay there with his hands behind his head and mulled it over for a minute or two, and then he told himself that maybe it was a good thing he'd wandered out of his daybreak rut before it was too late. *I am not a blind bear going back and forth in a cage*, he told the universe.

"Elizabeth?" he said. "Are you awake?"

"Yes. Yes, I am," she answered. "Good morning."

"Good morning," he said back. "How are you, Elizabeth?"

There was a silence, and Elizabeth propped herself up on one arm and stared at him. "What did you say?" she asked.

Henry's mind was still on Timmy; he'd heard her, but he wasn't listening. "Elizabeth," he said, "let's go someplace today and take Timmy with us."

She was still staring at him, holding the bedsheet clutched up against her chest with both hands, and he didn't like the expression on her face. *Say something, Henry,* he told himself. *So she'll know you haven't lost your mind.*

"I'm okay," he said. "I just suddenly realized, Timmy hasn't had a chance to go many places. And it's Sunday, so I don't have to go to work... Where could we take him?"

"How about the zoo?" she asked. "It's almost free."

Henry thought about bears and turtles, and he got a sick feeling in the pit of his stomach, but he told himself not to be such a fragile little flower. *I am not a fragile little flower.*

"Okay," he said, "the zoo it is!"

Elizabeth was smiling at him, morning light shining through her hair and in her eyes, and he tried to smile back. There was no reason why he should spoil her pleasure just because he knew this would surely be her last — and Timmy's only — trip to the zoo.

"The zoo," he said again, and added, "We have to take the bus. Ralph's still not through with the car."

"I like the bus," she said. "I'll go get Timmy up and start breakfast!" And she went off down the hall whistling a song he was sure he had once known the name of.

He'd been prepared to run into Joe on the bus; it didn't surprise him. It did surprise him when Joe waved one hand as he saw them but made no move to come bother them. *Well,* he thought, *two can play the botheration game!* He led Elizabeth and Timmy back to the seat in front of Joe and sat them down, and he slid in beside the homeless man.

"Morning, Joe," said Henry, and then he proceeded to make introductions... "Elizabeth, this is Joe; Joe, this is my wife Elizabeth, and this is my kid, Timmy; Timmy, this is

CHAPTER SEVEN

Joe" ...while they nodded and smiled. It was amazing, all that good will in one place, and the kid didn't even cry, not even when Joe reached over and patted his head. "And my name is Henry," he added, realizing that he'd never said so before.

"Mister Joe," the child asked, "are you going to the zoo, too?"

"No, son," the man said. "But I'm glad *you* are."

"Where are you going?"

"Timmy! Mind your own—"

Joe put a hand on Henry's wrist, hushing him.

"I'm just going about my business, Timmy," he told the child. "Going back and forth in the world on this bus, listening to people. It's what I do."

Henry made a rude noise. "You don't listen *much*, Joe!" he jeered. "Mostly you talk, and *other* people have to do the listening!"

The homeless man smiled. "Henry," he said, "talking and listening are all part of one thing; it goes around and around. They're the two ends of a loop, and you can't separate them."

"Hmmmmmph," said Henry, restraining himself; he didn't want to get too obnoxious in front of the child.

"Shall I tell you a story, Timmy?" the homeless man asked, and Henry jumped in with "See? See what I mean?"

But Timmy was only a child; he thought a story was a great idea, and said so.

So the homeless man began...

"Once there was a donkey who wanted to make friends with a pig. He walked right up to the pig and told her good morning, because that seemed like a good way to start. But the pig — which was a very large pig, by the way — only turned her back and showed the donkey her curly tail.The donkey thought, 'This pig must not have seen me! Or maybe this pig is a little bit hard of hearing!' He walked around the pig until he was standing in front of her again, to be sure she could see him, and he spoke up in a loud

voice to be sure she could hear him, saying, 'Good morning, Pig!' one more time.

"When the pig turned her back without a word and showed her tail again, the donkey was surprised. It didn't seem like the way a decent animal ought to treat somebody who only wanted to make friends. It seemed to him that this was not the way things were supposed to go, and that the rule was for the pig to say good morning in turn, without any whirling around. *But maybe I'm mistaken,* the donkey thought. He knew he'd grown up in a barn, and he'd never traveled, he knew he came from very plain folks. *Maybe this is the way it's done,* he thought. *Maybe this is how up-to-date animals get acquainted.* And so, afraid of seeming ignorant, he turned his back and matched the pig tail for tail.

"He waited and he waited to learn what the next step was in getting to be friends with fashionable and sophisticated animals. Time went by, and more time went by. Finally, he sneaked a look back over his shoulder. And there was the pig, rooting in the ground, clear over under the apple tree! She had just gone off without a word and left the donkey standing there."

The child had been listening hard, and he nodded his head. "The pig was the one that was wrong," he said solemnly. "Not the donkey."

Henry was amazed; he'd had no idea the kid could talk like that. To cover his surprise he turned to the homeless man and said, "Well? Isn't there a rule to go with it?"

"Yes. The seventh one," said Joe. "The Seventh Rule is: **TRUST YOUR INNER GRAMMAR.**"

"Well, you don't have to YELL!" said somebody two rows back, and somebody else said, "I don't GET it!" Henry realized that those were rituals, too; he'd never thought of it that way before.

"I don't get it either," he said carefully. "And I hate that word."

"Which word?"

CHAPTER SEVEN

"*Grammar!* Everybody hates that word, don't you know that? And your story doesn't make any *sense!*"

"Daddy," said Timmy, "can I tell you?"

Henry didn't like that; he didn't like that a bit. But he nodded his head and said yes.

"That donkey knew the right way to do it," said the child. "Okay? He knew how you start to be friends. He knew the *rules*, Daddy!"

"Absolutely right," said the homeless man, looking tremendously pleased. "That's all a grammar is — just some rules that go together. The rules for a game of football are its grammar. What's to hate?"

"That donkey should have just stuck to it!" Timmy went on happily, bouncing up and down in the seat. "He should have susplained!"

"EXplained, honey," Elizabeth said. "And don't bounce, please."

Henry was outraged. "How about when you're in Rome you do what the Romans do??" he demanded. "How about that?'

"It wasn't one of *them*, Daddy," Timmy said. "It was a donkey and a pig."

The idea that the child understood the stupid story and he, the man in charge here, didn't, was horrifying. Henry had to do something to get away from it. He stood up and snatched Timmy out of the seat, yelling, "Come on! We're gonna miss our *stop!*" And he didn't look back; he knew Elizabeth would follow him no matter what she thought. She always had.

The zoo was shady and cool, and the animals were interesting — even the bears and the turtles. Henry found himself feeling almost cheerful. Elizabeth and Timmy were having such a good time; he was glad he'd decided to bring them.

But Elizabeth spoiled it, of course. As usual. After a while, she said, "We ought to do this more often, don't you think so, Henry?"

"Why can't you just appreciate it *this* time, Elizabeth?" he said fiercely. "Why do you always have to go whining and begging for MORE?" *You're not what I expected, Elizabeth,* he thought bitterly, *not what I expected at all!* And he got ready for what he knew was coming. He had his lecture all ready. He had all his points lined up in a row, ready to teach her a lesson.

But she spoiled that, too. Instead of snapping back at him, which he would have been willing to accept as fair, she bent down and gave Timmy a hug and said nothing at all.

Henry couldn't just stand there and let that go by. "*Didn't you hear what I said?*" he asked her, his voice harsh and sharp.

"I heard you," she said, straightening up and looking him right in the eye, her hands rubbing Timmy's shoulders gently. "I heard you say you are really and truly tired, Henry. I heard you say it's been a long day and it's time we went home."

Henry swallowed hard and looked past her, as if he saw something interesting in the distance. "I guess that's what I meant," he said, mumbling the words. "I guess."

Later, while Elizabeth was putting Timmy to bed, he thought about skipping the Advent calendar. The day had been too full of surprises for him, including finding Joe sitting next to somebody else when they took the bus home and having to just say hello and go sit in the "Well, you don't have to YELL!" pews with all the other people. His stomach hurt him and his head ached, and he thought "I can't *face* it!" But he couldn't face ending the day without it, either. *I guess I **need** rituals,* he thought; it surprised him.

He opened the paper window and smiled at the little donkey he saw there. That would be the donkey that car-

CHAPTER SEVEN

ried Mary and the Baby to Bethlehem. Not the one that didn't even have enough confidence in himself to stand up to a pig.

Henry took out his pencil and covered up the donkey with gray.
Gently.

PEACETALK 101

CHAPTER EIGHT

Henry got to his office early the next morning, but the man at the next desk was already there working; he looked up, saw who it was, and went right back to it. Nelson, the man was called; Nelson something. *And last week, because of an argument that he wasn't even around for, I took his head off when he said goodmorning to me,* Henry thought. *That's pretty crummy of you, Henry. You and all your opinions about the way people badmouth each other and glory in it... how about putting your money where your mouth is?*

It wasn't a happy thought. Henry was sure that if he apologized he'd get zapped in return; that's how the game is played. That's what people do. *You'd live through that, Henry,* he told himself. *You won't live through next Sunday, but you'd live through another smart crack or two.*

"Morning, Nelson," he said cautiously. But then, although he'd had "I'm sorry" firmly in mind, what came out of his mouth next was "How's it going?"

Nelson looked at him, eyebrows raised, and said, "Whadda *you* care?"

Henry cleared his throat, took a deep breath, and answered. "The truth is, Nelson," he said slowly, "that I *don't* care how things are going with you. You're right about that. The truth is that I'm sorry I spoke to you the way I did last Wednesday, and I'm sorry I sat here all day

PEACETALK 101

Thursday and Friday and just let it fester. And because it's not easy for me to say this kind of stuff, I asked you a silly question. That's the truth."

It was, too — the whole truth.

Nelson looked at him hard, and Henry braced himself for the sarcastic remark he was sure was coming. After all, when you strip yourself naked without an invitation, you can't expect whoever's around for your performance not to whistle. But he didn't look away, in spite of how stupid he felt.

"Hey, it's all right," Nelson said, not sounding sarcastic at all. "Everybody gets up on the wrong side of the bed once in a while. No problem."

"Okay!" Henry said. He was surprised and pleased. (Somewhere inside his head, the voice said, *Reject preconceptions!*) "I'll try to keep a civil tongue in my head from now on."

"Wife giving you a hard time at home? Your kid got flu or something?"

"Naah." Henry sat down at his desk and reached for the stack of files. "It's my car. I need it this weekend, and the mechanic isn't getting anywhere with it. It's driving me nuts."

"You could always rent a car for a few days," Nelson said. "It doesn't cost all that much — they've got all kinds of special deals now."

The suggestion hung in the air; Henry felt the words like blows. *Rent a car. Do away with your wife and kid, in a rented car.* It made him feel sick. No way. What he had to do was horrible enough, without putting Elizabeth and Timmy in some strange car they'd never been in before. He would do it in his *own* car, where they were used to being. Maybe it didn't make a nickel's worth of sense, since they'd never know anyway, but for some reason it mattered to him. He had to do this thing. Even pets, if you were going someplace and you couldn't take care of them any more, you did what had to be done. And this wasn't pets, this was his wife and his kid. He had to do it, and he

CHAPTER EIGHT

had to do it *right.*

"Naah," he said, hoping his voice didn't sound as shaky to Nelson as it did to him. "Ralph's a good mechanic; he'll get it figured out in plenty of time."

When he got on the bus to go home that afternoon he saw Joe about halfway back, sitting beside a young woman whose eyes were a green God never meant eyes to be. Henry went down the aisle and took the seat behind them.

"Candy," Joe said to the woman, "you're sitting right in the hot sun. Does it bother you?"

"It does," she said. "It really does."

"There's a seat in the shade right up there," Joe told her, pointing. "You go ahead and take that one if you'd be more comfortable."

"Very neat," Henry commented as he moved into the seat where the woman had been.

"Thank you," said Joe.

"How do you always know exactly the right thing to say?"

The homeless man grinned at him. "I pay attention," he said. "I reject preconceptions. I stay in tune with whoever I'm talking to. I take no bait. I preserve face — mine and the other person's. I choose my metaphors, instead of just letting them fall on me. And I trust my inner grammar. That's how."

Henry snorted. "I should have known," he said.

"That's right. By now, you should have."

"Up to now," Henry said, "your rules have been okay. I guess. Sort of common sense. But you lose me with that 'inner grammar' garbage. I always got charity C's in grammar."

"What do you think grammar is?"

"Dangling gerundated past tense *participles,* man! Objects of the blankety-blank preposition! I mean, who knows that stuff? And who cares? NObody!"

PEACETALK 101

"Wait," said Joe. "Hang on a minute. Suppose somebody tells you a joke. What are you supposed to do?"

"Laugh. If it's funny. Say 'That's not funny', if it's not."

"You're not supposed to say 'I do'? Or maybe 'Six people can fit in the back of a Volkswagen?'"

"Well, of course not!"

"How do you know that?"

"Come on — everybody knows that!"

"Exactly!" Joe said, and the grin was even wider. "You use your inner grammar to make those decisions, and it never lets you down. Forget the dangling participles; just trust it."

Henry thought about that. And he thought about the fact that this morning his inner grammar had gotten him through the scene with Nelson without a hitch.

"If that's true," he said slowly, grudgingly, "if you can trust your so-called inner grammar, how come people keep ending up in dumb arguments over things they don't even care about?"

"You have to pay attention to which rules you use. The rules for getting into dumb arguments are in your inner grammar, too."

"Well, how do you know which one to *pick*?" Henry asked crossly.

"I know a story about that," said Joe.

"Once there was a teenager that wouldn't make her bed. Day after day her mother would remind her to make it; day after day she'd say okay. And day after day, when the girl had already left for school, her mother would go into the room and there her bed would be, not made. The day came when the mother was completely out of patience. She talked to her mother about it, and the grandmother agreed — she shouldn't put up with such behavior any longer. So when the teenager got home that day her mother met her at the door and said, 'YOU! YOU are the STUBbornest, most PIGheaded, most disoBEDient child I EVER KNEW! I have never even HEARD of a child

CHAPTER EIGHT

a s
rotten as you! You're going to be SORry, when you grow up and find yourself living in a DUMP, young lady! You'll NEVer get a husband, the way you act! And FURthermore...' The mother knew a lot of words; she went on like that for quite a long time.

"The next morning after the teenager had left for school again the mother went into her room, expecting to find the bed neatly made. But it not only wasn't made, the covers were on the floor and the pillow was clear across the room. The mother was flabbergasted. She went to her mother and told her what had happened.

"'Tell me exactly what you said to her,' said the grandmother, and she listened carefully to the whole long tirade, shaking her head. 'Now tell me exactly what you wanted to get across to her,' she said when it was over.

"'Well, for heavens sake,' said the mother, 'that's OBvious! I wanted to get it across to her that she has to make her bed!'

"'Hmmmph,' said the grandmother. 'Why didn't you try saying THAT?'

"Which brings me to Rule Eight," said the homeless man. "The Eighth Rule is: **CHOOSE YOUR COMMUNICATION GOALS.**"

Henry thought it over; he took his time. "The mother's communication goal," he said carefully, "wasn't to get the kid to make the bed, it was to make the kid feel like a creep. And for doing that, the mother chose the right rules. Right?"

The homeless man sighed a long deep sigh of satisfaction.

"My friend," he said, "you're starting to get it. You really are starting to get it!"

Henry felt like he'd won a prize or something; it was ridiculous.

"I'm not your friend," he said, to cover that up.

"Then you're picking all the wrong rules," Joe told him. "You should be using the rules out of the drawer labeled 'Talking To The Enemy.' Think about it. Because you know exactly what you're doing."

"I do?"

"People don't just jabber," said Joe, "although that makes a handy excuse if they can get other people to believe it. When people talk, they know what they're doing. They may not know *why*, but they know *what*."

Henry went to bed early, without looking at the Advent calendar, and was very satisfied with himself for having that much sense at last. But it didn't turn out to be that simple. It bothered him. He kept tossing and turning. When Elizabeth asked him if he had a headache, he seized the opportunity.

"Yeah!" he said. "You go on to sleep — I'm gonna go take some aspirin."

He went and got the calendar and took it in the kitchen, and sat down at the kitchen table with it. *Okay, Henry*, he told himself. *Don't be an idiot. Open it, so you can get some sleep.* If somebody had asked him which would be worse, seeing something from Joe's story, like all the other times, or seeing something that had nothing to do with the story, he wouldn't have been able to answer the question. But the very worst thing — so far — was not knowing what was in the window; that much he was certain about.

Window Eight had a picture of a bed, all nicely and neatly made, with plump pillows; the bedspread had a candy-cane pattern.

It took him a long time to cover it up with gray pencil, because all the little candy canes kept showing through.

CHAPTER NINE

Henry had been pretty sure that getting Ralph to come work on the car in the evening, after a long day at the shop, would be impossible; he only tried because he had so little time left. But because it was so important, he really put his back into it.

He paid very close attention to what Ralph said and to what he himself said back. He didn't leap to any conclusions about what Ralph would say; he rejected preconceptions right and left. He stayed in tune, speaking Ralph's language in every way he knew. When Ralph tried to provoke him, tried to get him going, he ignored it — he took no bait, no matter how tempting. He was careful to set things up in such a way that if Ralph finally did give in he wouldn't feel like he'd lost face. He talked about how a good mechanic is like a good doctor, and can save lives, choosing that metaphor because he happened to know that what Ralph had really wanted to do was go to medical school. He trusted his inner grammar to get him through the conversation. And he was careful to remember that the goal he'd chosen was not to *win*, or to make Ralph *lose*. The goal was to convince Ralph to come fix his car. It took a while, and keeping track of it all wasn't easy. You'd have to practice all that stuff, he realized, if you wanted it to be easy. But it ended with Ralph saying,

"Okay, buddy — just this once! I'll be there about eight."

Far out, Henry thought. *Joe would be proud of me.* Not that he cared what the homeless man might think about him, but it would have been neat if Joe could have been there and seen Henry, using the Rules to fly by, and making a perfect landing.

Ralph was as good as his word; he showed up at five minutes before eight, toolbox in one hand, beer in the other.

"Where's Timmy?" Ralph asked him as they walked to the garage.

"Already asleep," said Henry.

"Shoot. I was looking forward to talking to him again."

"I don't see how you can talk to a three-year-old kid," Henry grumbled.

Ralph raised the hood of the car and peered under it. "Easy," he said. "You talk while the kid listens, the kid answers while you listen, you talk while the kid listens, and so on. Like that. It goes around and around." He made going-around-and-around motions with his free hand.

"But—"

"Of course you've gotta speak the kid's language, you know! Three-year-old kids, they don't know anything about beer and poker and pretty women and stock markets. You use your common sense."

"Well, what *do* they know how to talk about?"

Ralph banged on something, hard, and reached for the flashlight on his hip. "You were three years old once, man," he said. "What did *you* talk about?"

Henry thought about it. "My mom, I guess. My dad. What my dad did at work. The kids I played with. Stuff like that."

"You see? You're not dumb, Henry, you just have to remember to use the brains God gave you."

There was a lot more thumping and banging, and Ralph added that thumping and banging was the

CHAPTER NINE

language you needed for communicating with engines.

"Are you getting anywhere?" Henry asked him.

"Sure. Piece of cake!"

The sentence that popped into Henry's mind, all ready to go, was: *Well, if it's such a piece of CAKE, Ralph, how come it's taking you so blasted long to FIX it?* He looked the sentence over, where it was all written out in his head, and he considered it. Suppose he said that: He'd be putting Ralph on the spot, backing him up against a wall where he'd feel like he had to defend himself. It came out of the drawer labeled "For Picking Fights With People" or maybe "For Making People Feel Stupid and Lose Face." *It was obviously not the way to get the car fixed.*

"That's good news, Ralph," he said instead. "Let me know if I can do anything."

Suddenly Ralph was looking at him, hard, and he hadn't cracked his head on the car hood when he straightened up fast like that; it was one of the mysterious things about mechanics, the way they never cracked their heads on the hood.

"Listen, Henry," the man said, "I want to tell you something. You need to talk to Timmy more, man, you hear me? If he doesn't have talks with you, how's he gonna learn to do that? And Henry, let me tell you — you need to cut out this 'I'll have conversations with him when he's older' stuff. The people we love, man — they're just here on *loan*... You never know how long God's gonna let you keep them."

Henry knew the rule for what to say back, if things had been normal; his inner grammar was humming right along. He was supposed to say, "Oh come on, Ralph! Little kids don't *die!*" But things *weren't* normal, and Timmy *was* going to die, and he couldn't do it like that. Instead, he slammed one fist into the palm of his other hand and said fiercely, "God shouldn't *let* little kids die! He shouldn't have made a world where they *have* to!"

Ralph stared at him, shaking his head slowly. He took a long drink of beer, and then he said, "Henry, when you get up in the morning and brush your teeth, you kill millions of little creepy crawlies in your mouth. They didn't do anything to deserve that, man; for all you know, they've got plans. But you just decide — as part of *your* plan — that you're gonna off them all!"

"So?"

"So, deciding when mouthbugs die is part of the job of being a human being. And deciding when human beings die ... including little kids, man .... is part of the job of being God." And he ducked under the hood again, and didn't hit his head.

Henry couldn't think of anything at all to say. He stood there while Ralph tugged and banged and shoved, all of it as mysterious to Henry as the doings of God, while the silence got longer and longer. He wondered if Ralph had always done so much of this heavy kind of talking, and he just never had noticed. Or maybe up to now Ralph had thought that staying in tune with Henry meant beer and poker and pretty women and the stock market, but now he'd decided a different tune was called for. *Maybe you come on so heavy yourself lately, Henry,* he told himself, *that a man as smart as Ralph can tell that you're getting weird. And then maybe he knows the kind of thing you say, in that situation.*

"Henry?"

Henry jumped; he'd been a million miles away. "Yeah, Ralph?"

"You see Joe on the bus today?"

"Oh, sure. He never misses."

"Well, did he tell you a stupid story today?"

Henry laughed. "Does he ever let a chance go by?"

"Well, let's hear it!"

Henry felt his face twist and his shoulders twist and he was glad Ralph couldn't see him. "I can't do that," he said stiffly.

"Why not?"

"I never told a story .... a story that wasn't a joke ... in my whole life, that's why! And I don't remember it

CHAPTER NINE

anyway."

"I don't believe you, man," said Ralph. "Cut the garbage and tell the story. It'll help me work."

Henry shrugged, took a deep breath, and began....

"Once there was a bumblebee that got up in a bad mood, and she was out flying around and taking out her mean on everything around her. She flew by a red rosebush covered with blossoms and green leaves, and she looked at it and said, 'Rosebushes! Who cares about an old *rose*bush? *I* don't! I don't care if you get mildew and blight and disappear, right where you stand!'

"And she flew past a row of tall corn and she said, 'STUPid CORN! Who needs YOU? I don't care if you shrivel up and turn brown, right where you stand!'

"And she flew by a tall pine tree, and she said, 'You think I care about you? No WAY! I don't care if you get struck by lightning and fall over, right where you stand!' And then she..."

He stopped. "Ralph," he said, "it goes on like that. You know how Joe's stories are. The bee flies by all kinds of stuff... I can't remember all of it. Sunflowers. Water lilies. You know. I don't want to go through all that."

"Uhuh," said Ralph. "I hear you. So cut to the ending, man. Just give me the gist of it."

"And at the end of the day the bumblebee, all worn out from badmouthing things, turned around to fly back home. She flew past the spot where the pine tree had stood that morning, and it had been struck by lightning and had fallen over, dead. She flew past the corn, and it had all shriveled up and turned brown. She flew past the rosebush..."

"Et cetera, et cetera," said Henry.
"The *end*ing!" Ralph insisted.

"And with each thing she passed, the bumblebee wept more and more tears, because she'd been lying when she'd said none of them mattered to her, and she had been lying when she said she didn't care. She was so torn with grief that she prayed she would drown in her tears and not have to bear her pain any longer — but that didn't happen. When she got to her nest the wind was blowing hard, and it blew all her tears away into the air, and she just had to go on about her business."

"Which...."
"Which? Which what?"
"Which brings me to the Ninth Rule. And the Ninth Rule is: **AVOID LIES.**"
Ralph chuckled. "Well, you don't have to YELL!" he said.
"Sometimes you do."
"Say what?" Ralph stood up and banged the car hood shut, rubbing his hands on a rag to get the worst of the grease off.
"Joe says sometimes you do have to yell, just a little. Once in a while."
Ralph grinned. "Joe is quite a guy," he said. "And this car is now quite a car. All fixed and ready to go!"
"Great," Henry said, because he really meant it about no rented cars, so it had to be a good thing, didn't it?
And "Come on in the house, Ralph, and I'll write you a check."

So there was a pine tree behind Window Nine! That was to be expected. It was an Advent calendar, a Christmas thing. Almost everybody's Christmas tree was either a real pine tree or a plastic one trying to *look* like a real pine tree. Of *course* there'd be a pine tree. "It doesn't mean a thing," Henry lied, right out loud, in his firmest and most confident voice.
From their bedroom, he heard Elizabeth's voice.

CHAPTER NINE

"Henry? Is something wrong? Were you calling me?"

"No!" he called back. "No, everything's fine. You go back to sleep."

And he took his pencil, and he *scribbled* over the tree. So hard that it made a hole in the paper where the treetop star would have been.

PEACETALK 101

CHAPTER TEN

Wednesday afternoon Henry's boss made him go to a special meeting that was even more boring and useless than the regular meetings. Listening to the "motivational speaker," Henry kept thinking how much better it would have been to bring Joe in and give him whatever they were paying her. Her name was Jackie, she knew how to power dress, and she was one of those women they call "perky."

All the time she was talking about The Need To Have A Life Agenda he fought the temptation to say "Hey, Jackie, let me tell you about *my* Life Agenda! I do useless work here in this building till Friday, so I'll get a paycheck Friday afternoon. Friday night I write checks for all my bills. Saturday I mail the bills and put out all the garbage. And then Sunday I kill myself, and my wife, and my kid. How perky does *that* make you feel?" Just to see the look on her face.

But he knew what would happen right after he got the brief kick from seeing her face turn white and her jaw drop open. She wouldn't say "Way to *go,* Henry! Folks, let's all give Henry a great big enthusiastic *hand!*" No, she would gasp and go "*Oh,* my *god!!!*" and then somebody would call the guys in the white suits to come and take him away to a rubber room. So he gritted his teeth and lived through the endless meeting one long weary second at a time.

He fell into the seat next to Joe that night without even looking around to see what other seats might be empty. "Thank god this day is over," he said, and he meant it. "I thought it was *never* going to end!"

"It's not over," the homeless man said. "It's only five-thirty, Henry."

"The *hard* part is over," Henry told him.

"That bad, huh?"

Henry nodded, leaned back in the seat, and closed his eyes.

"That reminds me of a story," Joe began, but Henry stopped him.

"You can tell me the story, Joe," he said, "but I want to talk to you about something else first. Before you do that."

"Fair enough... Go ahead."

Henry didn't open his eyes or sit up any straighter; he just talked.

"Last night," he said, "somebody told me that deciding when the germs in your mouth should die is part of the job of being a human being, and deciding when human beings should die is part of the job of being God. What do you think about that?"

"I'd say it myself," said Joe.

"Well, is there more to it? Didn't something get left out? I mean, the rule I use for the germs is 'first thing in the morning when I get up, last thing before I go to bed, and right before special occasions.' But I don't see what God's rule for people could possibly be. Because every time I turn on the tv, there sits another bunch of babies dying of starvation in Africa and looking out at me. The way God's doing that part of His job is just plain crazy. There's no *rule* there."

Joe gave him a long hard look, while Henry waited, and then he said, "Henry, God has a system. *With rules.* Let me tell you how it works. Everybody knows when they're going to die, my friend, and nobody dies before they're ready. And—"

CHAPTER TEN

That woke Henry up. He sat bolt upright and he protested. "Oh, come on! I asked you a serious question!"

"It's the truth,' Joe went on calmly. "I don't mean you know with your conscious mind that you're going to die on February 11th at 3:14 in the afternoon. If you knew it that way, you couldn't function in this world. But somewhere inside, you do know; we could say that your *soul* knows."

"Joe," Henry said urgently, 'I'm not really into souls, you know what I mean?"

But the homeless man went right on. "Everybody comes into this world with a program all laid out — a certain number of lessons to learn, a certain number of chores to do. When that's finished, you know it, and you die. But not before. God only has to do three things, Henry. He has to keep His system running. He has to step in on those very rare occasions when so many programs get tangled up together that gridlock happens. And He has to grieve over the way we struggle as we go along."

"I don't feel *one thing* for the germs on my teeth when I brush them!" Henry said belligerently.

"You're not God," Joe pointed out. "God pays attention. To every sparrow, and every germ, and everything that is."

Henry stared at him, eyes narrowed, brows knotted in a scowl.

Joe looked right back at him, and drew a giant X across his chest with one finger. "Cross my heart," he said.

"I don't believe one word of that," Henry declared. "Not one word!"

Joe grinned. "Fortunately," he said, 'God's job doesn't depend on what you believe."

Henry made a rude noise. His heart was pounding and his head hurt and he was sorry he had asked the question. The idea that God might have let him come into this world with a list of chores that included killing Elizabeth and Timmy was intolerable; he didn't trust God, but he still wanted God to be above doing something like that.

"Tell the story, Joe!" he said. "Please — tell the story."

"You don't want to discuss—

"Just tell the STORY!"

Two rows back, a woman said, "Well, you don't have to YELL!"

Henry whirled around to tell her off, but Joe put a hand on his shoulder and stopped him. "It's okay, Henry," he said. "It's okay. Here's the story."

"Once a woman had a lunch date with a friend. They were supposed to meet right in front of the bank at twelve noon exactly, but it got to be twelve-thirty and still the friend hadn't shown up. It happened that the friend was stuck in a traffic jam, but the woman didn't consider that possibility. *I knew she wouldn't show up!* she thought. *It's because I'm not fancy like the rest of her friends!* And when a man walked past her and smiled, she snapped at him: 'What are YOU smirking about??'

"The man hurried to get away from her, and as he hurried he was thinking *A woman like that, pretty like she is....she can't be bothered to be polite to a man like me. It's because I'm fifty.* He went up the stairs to his apartment, where his wife was waiting for him, and when she said hello and asked how his morning had been he answered, 'I've been busy, Elena! BUSY! Which is more than YOU can say, obviously Just LOOK at this place!'

"The wife blinked, and walked out of the room without a word. *He's tired of me*, she thought, hurrying down the hall. *It's because I've gained a little weight.* And when her daughter called to her — 'Mom? Can you come see what I've done?' — she yelled, 'Listen, I'm not the MAID around here!' The daughter nodded to herself sadly and thought, *She hates me. It's because I'm ugly.* And she kicked her cat.

"Meanwhile, back at the bank... The woman's friend had finally turned up, all out of breath and very sorry. She opened her mouth to explain, but the woman drew herself up and spoke in words like cubes of ice falling out of the tray. 'Don't say a word! I understand *perfectly!* It's such an honor to have lunch with you, I should be *grateful* for the chance to stand here an hour and wait for you to show up!

CHAPTER TEN

Right?'
"The friend had meant to say how sorry she was, but now it was clear to her that the woman had never liked her anyway. 'Right,' was all she said. 'Absolutely right.' And she turned around and went home."

"Which brings me to the Tenth Rule: **ANYTHING YOU FEED WILL GROW.**"

The homeless man stood up then and faced the back of the bus, and he raised his arms and raised his eyebrows and pointed his fingers straight up, like he was leading a choir. Two people were already starting to say "Well, you don't have to YELL!", but they only got through 'Well, you...' and faded away.

"Thank you," said Joe, and he sat down again.

"Anything you feed will grow," Henry muttered. "Big deal."

"Plants, animals, kids," Joe said. "You feed them, they'll grow. Everybody knows that. But it may not occur to them that the principle applies to lot of other things. Anger? Sickness? Misery? Love? You feed them, Henry, they will grow. The more you put into them, the more attention you pay, the bigger and stronger they will get and the faster and farther they'll spread. Attention is food, just like fruitcake is food. Give a kid fruitcake, that kid will grow; give anger your full attention, it'll grow, too."

"I don't get it,' said a woman behind Henry, and she tapped him on the shoulder. "Do you get it?"

But Henry was thinking so hard that he didn't hear her. He was remembering how the two sisters arguing over that stupid nickel had fed one another's anger; he was remembering how Elizabeth, when he snarled at her at the zoo, had refused to feed his anger and said, "I hear you saying you're tired" instead. He was remembering how Nelson, at the office, could have fed the bad feeling between them and had instead said it was okay, everybody gets up on the wrong side of the bed once in a while. It seemed to him that there was some very important clue here, something that mattered terribly that was just outside the edge of his understanding. He was so deep in thought that he rode a block past his stop and had to walk back.

When he walked into the kitchen, where Elizabeth was stirring something in a big pot, he found himself wondering what to say to her; he was beginning to think it mattered.

"Hello, Henry," she said, and she looked at him and smiled. Her hair was damp from the heat, and there were little curls of it across her forehead; she reached up with the back of her hand and shoved them all back. "You're early," she said. "That's nice."

A sentence popped into his head immediately: *I suppose you're going to say that I've got time to mow the blasted GRASS!* He could feel that sentence, balanced on the tip of his tongue, all ready to be spoken. He swallowed hard. *She might mean it, Henry,* he told himself. *There might not be a catch. She might just be glad to see you. How about feeding THAT? It's free.*

"I'm glad to see you, too, Elizabeth," he said cautiously. What would she say back? He'd left himself wide open.

"Dinner's almost ready, honey," she said.

When Henry sat down to open the tenth window that night, it was different. Always before there'd been something in the story — like a rose, or a donkey, or a turtle — and he'd been able to either expect it to turn up or be convinced that it couldn't possibly. But the story Joe had told today had been mostly people saying things to one another. He had no idea what might be in the window this time, and he had to admit to himself that he was curious.

He opened the little window and looked, and there it was, framed in the glitter: *a fruitcake.* In his head, he heard Joe's voice: 'Give a kid fruitcake, that kid will grow;

CHAPTER TEN

give anger your full attention, it'll grow, too."

He sat there a minute and thought it over. It was a stretch, he realized; it wasn't nearly as close as all the other times. Maybe the run was coming to an end. Maybe the next story would be about a pig and the picture in the window would be a pair of rollerskates.

Maybe he was going to get back the logical world he had always known.

"Well," he said severely to the silent kitchen, "I certainly hope so!!"

PEACETALK 101

CHAPTER ELEVEN

This one day, and three more; and then it will be over. When Henry woke up Thursday morning, with a strange feeling in his chest, that was his first thought. He sat up in bed and looked around the small room, and for the first time in many months he actually saw it. *I'm going to die in this room,* he thought, *and just **look** at it! Look how **ugly** it is!*

There was the bed his cousin Cleo had given them when she moved to California. The covers thrown back in a tangle because of the humid heat; the sheets faded by the hard water they were washed in and by time. There was the old rug that had been there when they moved in — blue once, maybe, lint-gray now — with the bare spot in the corner where Elizabeth used to sit and rock the baby. A dresser from WalMart; a beat-up bedside table; a lamp he'd made in shop class in highschool and gotten a C-minus on. Door to the closet; door to the hall; window to the outside world; curtains the same color as the rug. Henry looked at it all, and he could hardly believe it.

"Elizabeth," he said slowly, "has it always been this ugly in here?"

She sat up beside him, blinking with sleep. "What?"

"Why didn't we at least paint the walls?" he asked her angrily, hammering on his thighs with his fists. He hadn't been able to face living in this world, and now he wasn't sure he could face dying in this room. Maybe he'd do it in the livingroom? But he couldn't remember how the livingroom looked; for all he knew, it was even worse.

"Henry, are you talking to me," Elizabeth asked, "or are you talking to yourself?"

"I don't know," he told her. "I'm thinking."

He sat there dreading the day ahead of him. Tomorrow he'd get his paycheck and he'd have the bills to deal with. Saturday he'd have to get everything ready; the car was fixed now, but there were lots of little things he had to do. Sunday he had a full schedule, and there'd be no Monday. But *this* day stretched ahead of him like one of those movie scenes where the pioneers come up over a hill and there ahead of them is this desert that looks like it runs clear to the end of the world. *I'll paint the damn walls!* he thought. *I'll tell them at work that my back's gone out on me again. Never mind avoiding lies — next to what I'm getting ready to do, what's one more lie? And I'll come home early and paint the walls!*

Elizabeth would be expecting him to drive to work today, he knew that, but he couldn't do it. No way could he make himself get in that car.

"Elizabeth," he said as he headed for the bathroom, "I've got to clean the car up some before I can drive it anywhere. I'll take the bus the rest of this week."

He slammed the bathroom door behind him, cutting off whatever she was trying to say to him and making the bottle of shampoo fall off the shelf onto the floor. He picked it up, glad it was plastic. And then he looked at himself in the bathroom mirror, and shook his head.

"You're ridiculous," he told his dreary image. He turned the water on to warm up, and went to the door and opened it.

"Sorry, Elizabeth, didn't mean to shake the whole house!" he yelled, and closed the door again. Carefully. Gently.

CHAPTER ELEVEN

The homeless man was on the morning bus, and he waved at Henry when he saw him get on, but people were packed in so tightly that nobody could move; if Joe told any stories, Henry wasn't able to hear them. But the two o'clock bus Henry took for home was almost empty, it was just him and Joe and the driver and a couple of teenage girls headed for the swimming pool.

"You're early," Joe said when Henry sat down beside him.

"I'm going home and paint the walls in the bedroom," Henry explained. He opened the paper bag and showed the man the can of paint and the rest of the stuff he'd bought.

Joe leaned over and looked in the sack. "Venetian Primrose?"

"It's yellow," Henry said. "Kind of a bright yellow, like sunshine. I don't know why they call it Venetian Primrose."

"It's a happy color. Did your wife pick it out?"

It occurred to Henry then that maybe Joe would think he was a creep for not asking Elizabeth what color she'd like to have. *Avoid lies!* a voice said in his head. *Preserve face!* he said right back at it.

"Bright yellow is her favorite color," he said aloud. It was true; he was proud that he knew that.

And then he realized that he could do even better. "If I had asked her," he said, certain that he was right, "it's the color she would have chosen. Does that remind you of a story?"

"No," said the homeless man.

"Well, tell me one anyway," said Henry.

"You sure?"

"I'm sure."

"Once there was a widow who had two daughters named Ann and Sue. Ann was always good and obedient; she did her chores and kept herself nice; she got good grades, and helped her mother in every way she could.

Sue was different; so different that when she turned sixteen and ran away from home nobody was the least bit suprised. The mother cried for a week, and the police searched for a year, but Sue was gone. No more loud music; no more clothes borrowed without asking and then lost; no more shouting and cursing at the table; no more report cards all Fs and Ds; no more money stolen from the widow's purse — she was just gone.

"The years went by, and the widow almost never mentioned Sue except at Christmas, when she would always say to Ann, 'It seems so strange without your sister.' But Ann knew how her mother missed Sue, and how worried she was about her, and she felt a low fierce anger at Sue about that that never went away.

"And then one day when the widow and her daughter Ann had come to the end of another peaceful day and finished all the chores and were sitting out on the front steps to catch the cool air of the evening they looked up and there was Sue coming down the street toward them! She had gotten older and died her hair red and gotten a terrible frizzy permanent and she was dressed like a ragged floozy, but she still looked like Sue; they'd have known her anywhere. *So!* Ann thought. *She's hit the bottom of the barrel at last and come running back here! Now Mom will have a chance to tell her exactly what a sorry excuse for a human being she is!*

"But the widow turned to Ann and said, 'Glory be, Ann, darlin', you run in the house and call for them to deliver the biggest fanciest most expensive pizza they've got, so we don't have to waste one minute cooking and cleaning up the kitchen tonight!'

"'Mom, we already ATE!' Ann said. 'We can't eat twice in one night! That's a terrible wicked WASTE!' But her mother only patted her hand and said, 'Do it, please!'

"And then she turned back toward the street and stood up and held her arms out wide, with tears pouring down her face, and called out, 'Welcome home, beloved child!' and gathered Sue into her arms, frizzy red hair and all."

CHAPTER ELEVEN

"That's it?" Henry demanded. *I always say that,* he realized. But it was what he was thinking, and he stuck to it. "That's *all?*"

"Well, let's see," said Joe. "I could add 'and they all lived happily ever after', I guess."

"That's not even *your story*, Joe!" said Henry. "All you did was rip off the story of the Prodigal Son! What's the matter, are you tired?"

"I am a little tired," the homeless man said, "now that you mention it."

"Well, I think it was a neat story!" announced one of the teenage girls.

"What's a prodigal son?" asked the other one; and the first girl said, "Don't you know *anything?* I'll explain it to you later!"

Henry ignored them. "And there wasn't even a *Rule!*" he complained. First a ripoff story, one that never had made any sense even in the original version, and then no rule to go with it! Henry was feeling cheated.

"Which brings me to the Eleventh Rule," Joe went on, steadily. "The Eleventh Rule is: **REAL LOVE IS ALWAYS UNCONDITIONAL.**"

"What the dweeb does THAT mean?" demanded the girl who'd never heard the story of the Prodigal Son, and her friend went "AAAARGH!" and announced that it was really embarassing to be out in public with somebody so ignorant and not even smart enough to keep her mouth shut so people can't *tell* she's ignorant.

"So why do you keep going places with her?" Joe asked.

"Because I love her," said the girl.

"My point exactly," said Joe.

"Real love is always unconditional," Henry said slowly, trying it out. It felt funny in his mouth, and sounded strange in his ears. "That's a tough one."

"How about Elizabeth and Timmy?" Joe said. "They love you, Henry." And he added, "And they don't keep score."

The bus driver glanced back at them all and said, "Oh, come on, Joe! *Everybody* keeps score!"

Elizabeth and Timmy don't, Henry thought. *Joe's right. They don't do something for me and then expect me to do something for them, and like that. They just go on loving me, no matter what.*

It wasn't a thought that pleased him; it made him feel old and weak and confused.

"Elizabeth hasn't got Brain One," he told them all flatly. "She hasn't got *sense* enough to keep score. And Timmy's only a little kid. He doesn't know *how* to keep score!"

"Like I said," said the bus driver. "EVerybody — except little kids and airheads — keeps SCORE! That's how you get through the day! You scratch my back, I'll scratch yours!"

"Oh, Lord," said Joe, in a voice so full of sadness that Henry was startled, "Now I really *am* tired!"

And for the first time in all the time that Henry had been seeing him, the homeless man stood up and went to the door of the bus as it pulled over to the curb, and he got off.

"Hey!" Henry said. "Where's Joe going?"

"Whadda *you* care?" the driver challenged him. "He's got a right to get off, like anybody else!"

"I guess he has to...." Hemy stopped. Well, sure. Even a man with no home and no job and nothing to do but ride the bus and bother people is going to have to get off once in a while to look after his personal needs.

When Henry finished with the bedroom, it still had scruffy old furniture and curtains, and the rug was still lint-gray, but with the bright yellow walls it looked like an entirely different place. Elizabeth was just delighted, and Timmy stood with his eyes wide and sparkling and said "It's *nice,* Daddy! It's *nice!*"

CHAPTER ELEVEN

It *is* nice, Henry thought. He was glad he'd done it.

And when he opened the window on the Advent calendar later and saw the Raggedy Ann doll looking up at him, he just grinned, and took his pencil, and covered her up.

PEACETALK 101

CHAPTER TWELVE

When Henry woke up the next morning there was a moment when he didn't know where he was. And then he remembered: *I painted the walls in here yesterday... painted them the color of sunshine.* He liked the way the early morning light from the window picked up the color of the paint. Or maybe it was the other way around. Either way, it made a tiny dent in the grayness of everything else in his life. He took a deep breath — and winced as his back told him how it felt about what he'd done.

"Ouch!" he said. And then, "Blast!"

"Oh, no," Elizabeth said. "Is it your back?"

"Yeah. It's used to just sitting around all day every day, you know? It's not used to painting walls." And in his head he heard himself yesterday, telling the boss he'd hurt his back and had to go home. *As you sow so shall you reap, Henry,* he told himself. *Next time, avoid lies.*

Elizabeth sat up beside him, nudging him gently around so that she could get at the sore muscles, and began working the kinks out for him.

See, Henry, you didn't have to ask her, he thought. *She just went straight to it, without being asked.*

It bothered him — he wasn't sure why, maybe because they so rarely touched each other any more — and he pulled away from her. "That's enough," he said.

She took her hands away from him immediately and tucked them under the sheet, out of sight. "So, are you staying home?" she asked him.

"No way," he said. "It's payday!"

"But—"

"I'll manage," he said, getting up very carefully, holding his back as straight as he could and trying not to breathe. "Don't fuss, Elizabeth, I'll manage!"

At work it was just like any other day. Tedious. Endless. Irritating. Boring. Painful, because of his back. The pits, like always, no better and no worse, except for getting his check and knowing that it was the last day he'd ever have to spend like this. But he had a new problem: *Joe wasn't on the bus.* Not on the way to work. Not on the way home.

He was astonished to discover that he minded. Joe was just one more homeless guy, one more weirdo; it wasn't like he was a friend or a relative, or even a business associate. *Whadda **you** care if he doesn't show up, dummy?* he lectured himself. *This way, you don't have to listen to him! Count your blessings, buddy!*

But that didn't work; it didn't make him feel any better. For one thing, he'd gotten used to talking to Joe every day, and this last day on the job seemed incomplete somehow without that conversation. For another, Henry really wanted to hear the last of the twelve stories and find out what the Twelfth Rule was — he'd been counting on it. Even if it was stupid, it mattered to him.

As he was getting off the bus that afternoon he asked the driver, "Have you seen Joe today?"

"Joe who?"

"I don't know," Henry said. "Just Joe. Homeless guy, rides the bus all day long — rides it all night, too, for all I know."

"Black hair with a white streak in front? Has a beard? Wears green sweats? Talks your ear off?"

"That's him. Have you seen him today?"

CHAPTER TWELVE

"No. But he's probably strung out somewhere, or in jail. You know how those people are."

Henry was on the bottom step, just getting ready to put his foot down on the curb, but that stopped him. *You know how those people are.*

"HEY," yelled the driver, "you getting off or not? I've got a *route* to cover, you know, I can't just sit here all *night!*"

"Sorry!" Henry snarled, making it as nasty as he could manage, and he stood watching as the bus pulled away, wishing he'd had the guts to say something else, to stick up for Joe and explain how he wasn't just one of "those people," he was something else. Something special.

He had let the chance go by, the way he always let things go by. But what the heck could he have said? *The guy's magic, he tells stories and then whatever he was talking about in the story turns up in that day's window on my Advent calendar?* He could just imagine the reaction to that remark! And how was he supposed to explain what he was doing with an Advent calendar, in the middle of August?

He walked on home despising himself, with his shoulders sagging, still trying not to breathe, and when Elizabeth told him hello and asked what kind of day he'd had he just glared at her.

"Your back's really hurting you," she said. "I knew you should have stayed home."

"It's not hurting me!" he said. "I can't afford to have it hurting me!"

"What does *that* mean?" she asked, frowning a little.

"It means I have to write the blasted BILLS tonight, Elizabeth! I told you it was payday, can't you remember *anything*?"

He saw the hurt in her eyes for a second, before she lowered them and said, "I've got to go see what Timmy's up to," and left the room. And he was glad to see it. Good! He was hurting, bad; why should he be the only one hurting? *If I had a cat, I'd kick it!*, he thought. And then it occurred to him that he did have a dog .... at least, he *had* had a dog ... but he hadn't seen it for days.

"Elizabeth!" he yelled. "What have you done with the dog?"

When she didn't answer he went after her, and he found her in the tiny room — not much more than a closet, really, but they called it a room — where Timmy slept. She was on the floor with the child, helping him build some dumb thing with his stupid blocks.

"Elizabeth," he snapped, "I asked you what you did with the DOG!"

The little boy looked up at him, his eyes wide and hurt just like his mother's.

"Daddy," he said, "Scruffy *died.*"

*They hadn't even bothered to tell him. His own dog had died and they hadn't even cared enough to **tell** him!*

Henry was furious, with a cold hard rage that closed his throat tight and made all the muscles in his cheeks clamp down. It must have been obvious, because Timmy suddenly went around Elizabeth and sort of hid himself behind her. It made Henry even angrier, seeing that. What was he, some kind of monster, that his own kid thought he had to hide from his dad?

But the icy voice in his head wasn't going to cut him any slack about that. *You **are** some kind of monster, Henry*, it said to him. *You're going to kill him. Hold that thought, Henry. Try to keep it in mind.*

It was too much for Henry. He was trying, he was trying so hard! And nobody and nothing was helping. It had always been that way, sure, but it seemed to him that right now it should have been different. And *killing* ... That was the wrong word. He didn't feel that he deserved to have that word tacked on what he was doing. There should have been some *better* word, some word that made allowances for the fact that he was only doing what he *had* to do! Some word that didn't make it evil. It wasn't fair. He couldn't stand it.

"Well, good!" he yelled. "I'm *glad* it died! It never

CHAPTER TWELVE

minded me, not one single time did it ever mind me! It had *fleas*, and it was a *stupid* dog, and I'm *glad* it died! But somebody might have had the decency to TELL me!"

"Henry—" Elizabeth began, and the way her voice was shaking disgusted him; he cut her off.

"Don't bother me with your stupid excuses!" he spat at her. "I don't want to hear *any* of it! I've got to go write the *bills!*" And he slammed off down the hall to start tying up the loose ends of his sorry life, bellowing over his shoulder, "And I *don't want* anything to EAT!"

It was true; his stomach was a tight knot of fire inside him and the thought of eating made him sick.

By eleven o'clock the checks were all written. Including the one to the nursing home, to pay for some flowers for his mother on her birthday, with a card from him and Elizabeth and Timmy. She wouldn't know what day it was, or who *they* were; for all he knew, she wouldn't know what *flowers* were, by that time. But he wasn't going to have the people at that place saying he didn't care about his own mother. The envelopes were all addressed and stamped and stacked neatly on the kitchen table with a rubber band around them, ready to mail first thing in the morning.

Henry had turned down Elizabeth's offer of a sandwich. "Oh, please don't go to any *trouble,* Elizabeth!' he had sneered at her. "I wouldn't *think* of imposing on you!" And then, ostentatiously, making as much racket as he could, he had made the sandwich for himself, right in front of her, and choked it down. When she tried to talk to him he yelled at her; when she came in carrying Timmy, to tell him goodnight, he yelled at them both.

Through it all, he knew with absolute and bitter certainty that he was being cruel, that he had no reason to be cruel, that the way he was behaving was evil and that it made no sense; but he couldn't help it. He despised himself for that, too. *Hang in there, Henry!* he told himself grimly as the house grew quiet and dark. *Hang in there!*

It's almost over!

He took the Advent calendar out of his briefcase and laid it on the table in front of him, next to the stack of mail, but he didn't touch it. The whole day had gone wrong. It didn't seem to him that this day deserved to have its passing marked by the ritual of opening a window in its honor. A man has fallen about as low as he can fall, he thought, when he can't even deal with being stood up by a homeless weirdo pest.

He looked at Window Twelve, and he told himself he didn't care what was behind it. Why should he care? It didn't mean a thing.

Henry took his pencil and — very lightly — made a small gray question mark on the paper square that kept the tiny window closed; and then he stuffed the calendar back into his briefcase and went to bed.

CHAPTER THIRTEEN

Saturday morning finally arrived, and Henry woke up from maybe half an hour of uneasy sleep, feeling as if he'd been under water all night. It was like a dark flood was filling him up inside, rising up to his eyes and ears and brain, determined to drown him. Whatever it was, it had tides and surges and waves; it made him want to pound on the furniture and kick the walls and yell. But with the memory of last night's Frankenstein act clear in his mind, he thought it would be smart for him to try behaving like a normal human being for a while.

And just how are you going to pull that off, Henry? he asked his image in the mirror as he shaved. And it came right back at him with, *You've got to find a way — or you'll scare Elizabeth so bad that she'll haul herself and Timmy right out of here, the way desperate battered women do.*

Henry had never struck Elizabeth, or even shoved her out of his way. The way he felt about it was simple: No real man would hit a woman. Not unless she was stark crazy and standing over him with a butcher knife, and even then you'd hit her as gently as you could. It seemed to him completely unfair that his wife, who had no idea that he planned to kill her and their child, was afraid of him. What had he ever done to deserve that?

He wished there were some kind of anonymous

PEACETALK 101

telephone counseling service he could call to ask that question. There ought to be. There ought to be people you could ask the really hard questions and get useful answers, if you were really — like Joe said — supposed to carry out a program while you were here. That would be fair. (Not that he believed stuff like that.) But fair or not, he knew he had to be careful today. He didn't have the excuse of a long day at work with an aching back to get him off the hook.

Work, he thought. Hard work was what he needed. He'd mow the yard. Why not? Maybe fix the board on the porch that was sort of sagging when you stepped on it, the one that worried Elizabeth because she was scared it would break and somebody would get hurt. He could wax the car. That kind of stuff. It would pass the time and keep him from putting his fist through a window or something equally loony. But first he had to mail the bills.

And maybe do just one more thing.

He took the stack of envelopes and walked down the street to the mailbox and stuffed them in. And then he went on down the street one more block to his regular bus stop, and he stood there and waited till he saw the bus go by.

Joe wasn't on it.

Henry went back home, thinking hard. He went out to the garage and found the can of car wax and dropped it in the garbage, shoving it way down where nobody would see it unless they were really looking for it. And then he went in the house to look for his wife, calling, "Elizabeth? Elizabeth, where are you?"

"I'm right here," she said at his elbow, making him jump. He wished she wouldn't sneak up behind him like that. He'd told her a thousand times.

"I want to wax the car," he said, "but I'm out of wax. I've got to go to the store and get some. I'll be right back!" And he was out of there, walking fast, back to the bus stop.

CHAPTER THIRTEEN

The bus came; no Homeless Joe. Henry rode it to the store, got off and bought the wax, and caught the next one going back. Still no Joe. As the bus pulled up to his stop he walked to the front, leaned over the driver and spoke to her.

"You know Joe?" he asked her, trying to sound casual. "The homeless guy?"

"Yeah, I know him," she said. "So? Make it quick, it's against the rules to have conversations with the passengers."

He handed her the business card and she stared at it. It was a faded yellow, and wrinkled, and it had a spot of catsup right next to the zip code.

"Don't *use* these much, *do* you?" she said.

Henry shook his head. He'd never see her again, and he didn't have to worry about what she thought. When he'd ordered the cards, he'd really believed there might be some hope in his idea for a home business, something he could use to get himself and his family out of the pit they were in — but he wasn't going to tell her *that* sorry tale. "I've been carrying that one for a year," he said, "and I've never needed it yet."

"So what am *I* supposed to do with it?'

"If you see Joe, will you give that to him and tell him I need to get in touch with him? And tell him it's urgent?"

The driver shrugged. It was no skin off her nose, she assured him, and she stuck the card in her shirt pocket and told him to get off, for crying out loud, and he did.

She might throw the card away the minute he was out of sight. She probably *would* do that. But he couldn't think of anything else to try. Finding Joe was out of the question. There were a hundred places, underneath bridges and out along the gullies by the railroad tracks, in flophouses and down dark alleys, where the homeless hunkered down. You could hunt for days and never find the person you were looking for. Maybe she'd keep the card; maybe she'd see Joe; maybe she'd give it to him; maybe Joe would follow up on it. It was a lot of maybes; maybe pigs fly. But it was all he could come up with.

Henry worked his way doggedly through the long day, listening hard for the phone, or a knock at the door. He waxed the car till it shone like something precious. He mowed the yard, even in the places where he usually didn't bother, which meant he had to go get the rusty weedwhip and whack off the tall stuff before the mower would cut it; it was a pain in the neck, but he did it. He fixed the board on the porch, too. It was the kind of job he wasn't any good at, but he managed to make it so you could jump up and down on the spot where the broken board had been and it didn't budge. He worked all day long, trying to make the endless hours go by. And every once in a while he'd say to himself, *Pay attention, Henry — this is the last real day of your life!*

Because he sure wasn't planning to sit around Sunday and wait for a signal from the Suicide Fairy; he planned to get up and get it over with as fast as he decently could. And although it made no sense to pay attention now — you paid attention to stuff you might want to do something about later, and he wasn't going to be around that long — he kept noticing things.

He noticed that Elizabeth and Timmy both had the same identical crazy crooked part in their hair, tacking off across the top of their heads. He noticed that Elizabeth had put a bright red pillow on the livingroom couch that not only didn't match the rest of the room, it clashed with it viciously, and it made him grin. She had no more color sense than a blind man, and it was just luck that her favorite color was sunshine yellow and not the color of baked liver. He noticed, after he'd mowed the yard, that there were some zinnias in the flower bed she'd put in last spring that were ready to bloom. He noticed that when Timmy said 'rabbit" now he could say the R just as well as

CHAPTER THIRTEEN

a grownup. And he knew the sentence that went with noticing all those things. His inner grammar, his Rule Book, provided him with it. He was supposed to say to himself, *These are things that I will always remember.* Except that his dictionary had been changed. For him, "always" now meant "until maybe noon tomorrow, give or take a couple of hours."

After dinner, even after he had to put up with Elizabeth's father dropping in with another of his crazy ideas, there was nothing left for Henry to do. The next day loomed up ahead of him like the mouth of hell, gaping wide and black and grotesque, with flames and fumes pouring out of it — at least, that was what he would have said it was like if anybody had asked him. Up to now Sunday's schedule had been just a plan, just something abstract off in the future, something he told himself was coming but that seemed far away in an imaginary distance. Now that it was almost upon him, it was suddenly real, and it scared him to death. His heart pounded, and he broke out in a cold sweat, and Elizabeth told him he didn't look well and ought to go to bed early.

He shook his head. "No," he told her. "I'm not going to bed early. I'm going to clean the refrigerator."

Her mouth fell open in an expression he found especially unattractive, and she dropped into the closest chair as if all the breath had been knocked out of her.

"Henry," she said quietly, "have you lost your mind?"

He thought it over. There were a lot of things he could say. Like *Well, it's clear to me that YOU'RE never going to clean it, Elizabeth!* Or, *You know, Elizabeth, the maid doesn't DO refrigerators.* Or the old standby that had been his father's favorite: *Well, SOMEbody's got to do it, and I don't see any volunTEERS, do YOU?*

But he couldn't manage any of those sentences. They were all from the "For Talking To The Enemy" drawer. Elizabeth wasn't the enemy. She bored him, and she had disappointed him badly, but she wasn't the enemy.

He settled for "I'm gonna clean the refrigerator, Elizabeth. And I am not going to *argue* about it!"

Clear up to the last minutes before midnight, he kept hoping. The last bus didn't come out this way until 11:15, and it went far enough out that Joe'd know he had time to get off and stop by Henry's place and still be able to catch it on its way back downtown. He kept listening for the phone or the doorbell; he kept going to the front window and staring out into the dark. But when it got to be five minutes to twelve he understood that the card hadn't worked — or the bus driver had thrown it away, like he'd been afraid she would do — and Joe wasn't going to show up. *You see,* he said to himself sternly, *the universe is trying hard to tell you something. It's trying to tell you to give UP, Henry!* And he thought that if he'd been able to see inside himself, where the part of him that was supposed to think and dream was, it wouldn't be sunshine yellow in there. It wouldn't be Venetian Primrose. It would be exactly the color of baked liver.

Henry was an orderly and methodical person; that was one reason he'd ended up in a boring job next to the man named Nelson, who was also orderly and methodical. So, even though it made no sense, he took the Advent calendar out of his briefcase, took the pencil from the mug on the kichen table, and once again he drew a neat question mark. On Window Thirteen.

And then he went to bed and lay all night staring up at the ceiling, while the tapes played in his head.

CHAPTER FOURTEEN

Because he hadn't slept at all, there was no waking up for Henry Sunday morning. And there was no thought of "Here we go again!", because what he had ahead of him this day was a first. But *"I can't face it I can't face it I can't face it!"* was running through his head like the mad racket of a runaway train.

A hundred times he had called himself a coward, through that long night. A hundred times, methodical and orderly, he had gone over the list of reasons why death was in fact the best choice he had, both for himself and for his family. The reasons hadn't changed in any way, they were exactly what they'd always been. Elizabeth hadn't become a fascinating and independent and sophisticated woman who'd be able to look after her own self or snare a wealthy second husband to do it for her. Timmy hadn't turned into the kind of wonderchild he'd planned on having, the kind people would just naturally go out of their way to take care of. His job hadn't been transformed into neurosurgery or scientific research or orchestra conducting. His dog was still dead, his home was the same dingy crackerbox it had always been. The world was still the same drab and hopeless place, a wicked joke that some divinely evil force was playing on human beings. Nothing had changed. But this was going to be harder than he'd expected. He'd expected that by now he'd be eager to get it over with. He'd thought he would be used to the idea by now.

Be a man for once, Henry! he taunted himself as the morning light began to come through the bedroom windows and it was at long last time to get up and start this final day. *You've failed at everything you've ever decided to do, just like your father told you you would, you've settled for second best or tenth best or worse, every single time. Do what you know must be done, for once, and do it right!*

The thought that he might screw this up too was unbearable. *Don't you let that happen, Henry!* he yelled at himself. *Just DON'T let that happen!*

He slipped out of bed and pulled on a pair of jeans and a teeshirt and went down the hall to the livingroom, his bare feet sure and silent, and got his briefcase from the front closet and checked it.

Yes. His stash of pills, disguised by bottles that had held the pills prescribed for his chest colds and his back pain, was still there. He opened one of the bottles and took out three of the red capsules — one for Timmy, two for Elizabeth, surely enough to put them soundly to sleep — and shoved them deep into his pocket where they'd be easy to get to. He started to put the briefcase away, and then he stopped. *What if two capsules wasn't enough? What if...oh god, what if Elizabeth woke up while he was putting her and Timmy into the car? What if she woke up after he'd shut the car door and gone away into the house, before the carbon monoxide could work?* One more, he thought, *just to be safe*, and he put that in his pocket too. And in the other pocket he put the Advent calendar, because in his whole life it was the only thing even faintly magical that had ever come his way. He wanted it with him where he could touch it for luck, the way he'd seen people rub a rabbitfoot, for luck.

Next, he took a glass of orange juice and one of those stupid little cardboard boxes of cereal ...Choco-Yummies, or

CHAPTER FOURTEEN

some such thing... to Timmy's room and gave it to the child along with a picture book to look at. And he made a pot of coffee and took a cup of that and two slices of buttered toast to Elizabeth on the metal tray she always used when one of them was sick in bed.

She sat up when she saw him coming with the breakfast, and her eyes lit up and she clapped her hands the same way Timmy had clapped his. "Breakfast in bed for my birthday!" she said happily. "Thank you, honey!"

Her birthday. Henry would have dropped the tray if she hadn't reached out quickly and caught it as it tipped. *I didn't know!*

But that was a lie. Of course he had known. Some part of him, not necessarily the part Joe had called the soul, but some hidden part, had known. *You want me to remember your birthday, Elizabeth?* that part of him had ranted, mean as a snake. *Okay — I'll remember it! I hope you're happy with my birthday surprise!* He had always thought that he was not a mean man; it came to him now that perhaps he had been wrong about that too.

"Happy birthday, Elizabeth," he managed to choke out, and she thanked him again. And then he went on with the plan. He told her how he'd settled Timmy. He told her he was going to make brunch for all of them later. Elizabeth loved brunch; she thought waffles at eleven o'clock in the morning were exotic.

He left her happy, busy with her breakfast, wishing that as long as he was playing stupid games with his mind he had also bought her a birthday present. But then he shook his head. No, whatever that was inside him, it had made the right decision. A present would have made Elizabeth suspicious, because he always had to go get her something when the package from her father arrived — late — and reminded him. A present that turned up on its own, without that reminder, would have made her wonder if he was up to something, and that wouldn't do. Henry wanted her serene and relaxed when she started drinking the concoction he was going to dissolve the pills in, so she'd swallow it before she noticed that it tasted funny. He'd picked out the ingredients carefully: pineapple juice, papaya, and cocoanut. It would be strong enough, and strange enough, that she'd drink it in spite of the taste, because she wouldn't want to hurt his feelings. And so would Timmy drink the little glass that had just the one pill in it, and for the same reason.

He couldn't think about it any more, he realized. He had to do something to take his mind off it. "I'll be back in half an hour!" he called to Elizabeth, and he went outside, gulping the morning air in spite of the way it smelled. He would have liked to run, but he didn't dare. *You're so out of shape, Henry, if you ran you'd probably have a heart attack and miss your own suicide!* He settled for a brisk walk instead, and headed for the bus stop. He did break into a run, though, when he saw the bus coming, because if Joe was on board he wanted to get on, and there weren't many buses on Sunday.

But he didn't make it to the corner. To his astonishment, the driver honked and waved at him to stop, the bus pulled over to the curb right there in the middle of the block — something he knew was at least forbidden and probably against the law — and a little boy hopped off the bus waving a piece of notebook paper folded up small.

"Hey!" the kid said. "You're Henry, right?

Breathing hard, Henry admitted that he was.

"The driver *said* you were him! And Joe, he gave me a dollar to give you this and tell you he wishes you a good morning!" He shoved the piece of paper into Henry's hand, hopped back on the waiting bus, and was gone. The whole thing had taken about twenty seconds.

Henry opened the piece of paper with his hands shaking and his heart pounding, and he saw the words "Once there was…"

That was enough. He folded it back up, put it in the pocket where he'd put the Advent calendar, and went

CHAPTER FOURTEEN

straight home.

Sitting at the kitchen table, hearing Elizabeth and Timmy talking in the little boy's room about some fool thing Timmy was doing, Henry opened the paper all the way, laid it on the table, smoothed out the wrinkles carefully with both his hands, and read the story.

"Once there was a man named Henry, and he had a hard row to hoe. He wasn't happy; nothing about his life was the way he had thought it would be, and nothing he'd tried to do had ever gone as well as he had meant it to go. The day came when Henry knew he just couldn't stand it any more, and he made up his mind to get some pills and put a garbage bag over his head and end it all.

"And there was more. Henry wasn't the kind of man who made messes and then walked away and left them for somebody else to clean up. He was a man who took his responsibilities very seriously. He had a wife and child that he was sure nobody else would be eager to look after when he was gone, and he decided he'd end their lives too, before he took his own. And he made up his mind to go on for two more weeks, to earn one more paycheck, so he could leave his affairs in order, and he pulled himself together to get through those fourteen days somehow.

"But during those fourteen days Henry learned a lot of things he hadn't known before.

"He learned that when you pay attention to what other people say, when you really listen and don't decide what they're going to say before they even open their mouths, they often surprise you.

"He learned that although the world is full of people saying cruel and ugly things, that's mostly because other people are doing the same — if you don't feed all that cruelty and ugliness, if you don't take the bait coming at you, if you're willing to see to it that they don't lose face, they'll give that up and talk decently.

"He learned that you don't have to tell lies, because

there's always something true you can say instead.

"He learned that you can trust the grammar in your head to tell you the right thing to say; you just have to pay attention to what you're doing and pick the rule that's best.

"He learned that if you make an effort to stay in tune with other people you can have conversations instead of fights; he learned that when you choose your metaphors and your communication goals instead of just doing any old thing that pops into your head, you can have peace instead of conflict.

"He learned that real love is unconditional and doesn't keep score, the same way rain falls both on people who deserve it and people who don't.

"And when he put all of that together, and saw the world that way, he realized that most of being miserable was up to him all along, and so was most of being happy, and he decided that although the world wasn't perfect he could face living in it after all — and Henry changed his mind.

"Which brings me to the Twelfth Rule. The Twelfth Rule is: **JOY IS THE SKILL OF SKILLS**."

Henry wasn't crying, but he thought he might be any minute; he felt like his chest was going to burst. Trembling, he took the Advent calendar out of his pocket and laid it on top of the notebook paper, and drew a careful question mark on Window Fourteen. And then, one by one, he opened all three windows that were still closed

In Window Twelve there was a shiny round red Christmas tree ornament, and written on it in gold was the letter **J**.

In Window Thirteen there was a gleaming green bell — and a golden letter **O**.

CHAPTER FOURTEEN

In Window Fourteen there was a glorious bright silver star — and a golden letter **Y**.

They looked up at him, the three open windows, and they spelled one golden word: **JOY!**

He was so focused on that word that the tug at his elbow made him jump.

"Daddy?" Timmy said. "I made you a picture!" And he laid another piece of paper on the table, over the Advent calendar.

Now Henry *was* crying. Timmy had never made him a picture before. He looked at it. And he looked at it again. It was a brown blob. Just a brown blob, with a bump or two on it. It reminded him of several things, but none of them was anything he would have wanted to put up on the refrigerator door.

Carefully, he said, "Timmy, I can tell you really worked hard on this picture, and I thank you very much for painting it for me. It makes me very, very happy."

The little boy smiled at him, shoving both hands into his pockets. "It's a potato," he said. "Isn't it a nice one, Daddy?"

"It's a potato? A *potato?*"

Henry didn't recognize the voice that said that. Maybe it belonged to the part of him that had pretended it didn't know this was Elizabeth's birthday.

Timmy sighed happily. "Potatoes are the very best thing I draw, Daddy," he said.

Henry stood up, banging his shin on the edge of the table. *I'm going to have to find a way to stop shaking,* he thought. He gathered Timmy up into his arms and kissed him right on the top of his head. With his free hand he stuffed the three pieces of paper back in his pocket, where they'd be safe, and he threw the handful of pills from his other pocket down into the silent black welcoming maw of the garbage disposal. Holding Timmy tight, laughing through his tears, he ran out of the kitchen and down the hall, yelling at the top of his lungs. *This,* he thought, *is what they mean when they say* **shout for joy!**

"Elizabeth!" he yelled. "ELIZabeth! Come ON, honey, we're going out for brunch! And then, after that, we're going to the ZOO! COME ON, Elizabeth!"

Sometimes, he thought, as she came running, *sometimes you really do have to yell.*

THE END

ABOUT THE AUTHOR

Suzette Haden Elgin was born in 1936, grew up in the Ozarks, spent a number of years in California as a linguistics professor, and then retired to theOzarks again, where she runs the Ozark Center for Language Studies (a virtual business) from her home. She writes both fiction and nonfiction.

Her best-known titles are the
Gentle Art of Verbal Self-Defense book series,
her book on grandmothering
The Grandmother Principles
and her science fiction novels.

She has a homepage for **Peacetalk 101**
online at http://www.sfwa.org/members/elgin/ Peacetalk101/Index.html
with discussion questions, FAQ,
a mini-workbook, and more.
She would welcome your visits
there and any comments
or suggestions that you
might have about the material.
She can also be reached by mail at
    P.O. Box 1137
    Huntsville, AR 72740-1137.

YOUR NOTES

YOUR NOTES

Printed in the United States
18183LVS00002B/748